AF575698

NOVELS BY **BURT WEISSBOURD**

Callie and Cash Thrillers

Danger in Plain Sight

Rough Justice

Out of the Past

Corey Logan Thrillers

Inside Passage

Teaser

Minos

In Velvet

(a thriller set in Yellowstone National Park)

Danger in Plain Sight

"Here's what happens when you enter Mr. Weissbourd's world: You can't get out. You will be astonished not only by the colorful, playful, lethal characters, you will be hooked into a plot that laughs at whatever else you thought you were doing today. Callie and Cash, beauty and the beast, and the characters that swim through their world are each a gem of humanity observed."

—**David Field**, screenwriter and former head of West Coast Production United Artists

"Weissbourd delivers a polished page-turner about terrorism, money laundering, and the price of sins rooted in avarice."

—***BlueInk Review***

"From the author of the brilliant Corey Logan Trilogy, *Danger in Plain Sight* is the latest thriller from Burt Weissbourd and his finest novel yet. Weissbourd has created an entire genre—*Seattle Noir*. Callie James and her son, Lew, are indelible characters. I devoured the novel in a single night–and I think you will, too."

—**Jacob Epstein**, writer and executive story editor *Hill Street Blues*, writer *LA Law*

"A woman gets in touch with her inner action hero in this bracing thriller."

—***Kirkus Reviews***

Inside Passage

"A narrative that is relentlessly taut and exciting."

—***Foreword Reviews***

"*Inside Passage* hit all the hallmarks of a great read… Riveting story from the first paragraph."

—***Nightly Reading***

"The family dynamics and insights to human behavior had me reeling…. Juicy, fascinating stuff."

—***The (Not Always) Lazy W***

"*Inside Passage* is a great thriller and the restaurants you include as part of the story: Canlis, El Gaucho, Tulio, Queen City Grill, Wild Ginger, are all very sexy places. You really captured our city!"

—**Scott Carsburg**, James Beard award winner
and legendary Seattle chef

"I got completely hooked on *Inside Passage*""

—**Nancy Guppy**, host of *Art Zone* on Seattle Channel

Teaser

"A stunning, fast-paced thriller."

—***Roxy's Reviews***

"Burt Weissbourd is such a great writer... Such a great book!"

—***So I Am a Reader***

"Weissbourd, a seasoned screenwriter and film producer, has the mechanics down pat. Teaser is a fun, action-filled ride."

—***Foreword Reviews***

"Weissbourd's stellar writing, memorable characters and an extremely well-crafted narrative never disappoint."

—***Discerning Reader***

Minos

"Original, consistently compelling…Minos is an exceptionally entertaining and engaging read from beginning to end."

—***Midwest Book Review***

"These books transcend the expectations of genre fiction to become literature."

—**Jacob Epstein**, writer and executive story editor of *Hill Street Blues*, writer *LA Law*

"Mr. Weissbourd draws you into a world of characters and stories that keep you riveted, and you're pretty sure you are visiting people and worlds that have little or nothing to do with you. But he keeps going deeper, and by the end, he has delivered you back to yourself, a self you may not have admitted to before. Mr. Weissbourd, please keep writing."

—**David Field**, screenwriter and former head of West Coast Production United Artists

In Velvet

"This thrilling novel has a breathless pace that combines science and nature to create nail-biting tension."

—Foreword Reviews

"*In Velvet* left me breathless, a bit contemplative, and completely satisfied."

—Manic Readers

"Weissbourd's writing reminds me of the great Raymond Chandler mysteries."

—**John McCaffrey**, *KGB Bar Lit Mag*

"*In Velvet* is a thrill from start to finish!"

—Closed the Cover

OUT OF THE PAST

BURT WEISSBOURD

OUT OF THE PAST

A CALLIE AND CASH THRILLER

BLUE CITY PRESS
ISLIP, NY

RARE BIRD
LOS ANGELES, CALIF.

THIS IS A GENUINE RARE BIRD | BLUE CITY PRESS BOOK

Rare Bird Books
6044 North Figueroa Street
Los Angeles, CA 90042
rarebirdbooks.com

Blue City Press
62 West Bayberry Road
Islip, NY 11751

Copyright © 2024 by Burt Weissbourd

TRADE PAPERBACK ORIGINAL EDITION

Jacket design by Lisa Fyfe
Man Silhouette: Gantas Vaičiulėnas
Man Astrid Sosa

All rights reserved, including the right to reproduce this book or portions thereof in any form whatsoever, including but not limited to print, audio, and electronic. For more information, address:
Rare Bird Books Subsidiary Rights Department
6044 North Figueroa Street
Los Angeles, CA 90042

Printed in the United States

10 9 8 7 6 5 4 3 2 1

Publisher's Cataloging-in-Publication Data available upon request.

For my grandchildren:
Colin Weissbourd, James Weissbourd, and Asa McWeiss

Author's Note

Not long ago, Sara appeared, unannounced, in Callie's restaurant, Le Cochon Bronze. She said that she had a life-changing story to tell Callie's partner, Cash Logan.

As they listened, spellbound, Sara told how she grew up in an orphanage, escaped at ten, found her mother at fourteen, lived with her on a boat until her mom died five years later, went on to live with an American man in Paris, a martial arts instructor, who taught her how to fight expertly. Six years later, she spoke four languages, wanted to immigrate to America, and, against all odds, got a visa.

She arrived in Seattle to start her new job in the San Juan Islands. On the boat, the woman who picked her up at the airport tried to kill her. Sara, a capable fighter, drowned her, then set fire to the boat and blew it up. She knew no one in this new country, but she still had a letter that her mother had given her before she died. This letter was from her father—who never knew she existed—Cash Logan.

Over the next year, Cash, Callie, and their best friends—Andre, a prosthetic-legged Afro-Caribbean man, a mercenary, and a frequent partner in Cash's international import business; Itzac, the "Macher," one of the largest traders of diamonds in the world, a brilliant thinker, and Cash's mentor; Seattle Detective Ed Samter, a dear friend who'd been their staunch ally since Callie and Cash were in danger—all collaborated to save Sara's life.

To accomplish that, this unconventional team of highly functioning, unexpected friends hijacked a yacht carrying Sara's would-be killers, delivered them to prison in Cuba, then recovered $75,000,000 in stolen Cuban government money that the would-be killers had skillfully laundered out of the country, and finally, got Sara's identity back.

Today, eighteen months later, Sara is married to a Cuban, Alvaro, and they have a three-month-old baby, Cash's grandson, called Young Cash or simply Baby Cash.

This is where our story begins, as, inexplicably, Cash is troubled, depressed, irrationally angry with his friends, and worried unaccountably about the safety of his daughter and grandson.

Prologue

Cash and Callie sat at their preferred table, secluded in the far corner of the bar upstairs. From their spot, they could look across the magnificent brass-and-mahogany bar—a bar she'd acquired hastily, twelve years ago, from a quarreling couple in a tiny café in rural France. The husband had run off with a back-packing Laker girl, and his wife had put their bar up for sale that very day. Callie had hurriedly shipped the magnificent bar to Seattle, intact, before she'd even chosen the site for her restaurant. She'd never looked back. Today, from that bar, she could look down to the restaurant below where light tawny-tan wood tables and chairs were carefully set on dark mahogany floors. Tonight, the tables were gracefully covered with light grey linen tablecloths. Callie liked to look down over the beautiful dining room, check out how the evening was going. At the moment, it was quiet, warm, and pleasant downstairs in the restaurant.

Upstairs, they were eating their favorite dinner—Copper River salmon for Callie, cassoulet with game sausages for Cash. She had a fine white wine. Cash, uncharacteristically, sipped a single malt scotch, Glenmorangie, neat. She was thinking out loud, rambling about Lew's seventeenth birthday, a surprise party she and Lisa, Lew's girlfriend, were planning for him here in the restaurant. "Lisa is really in charge," she explained. "She's already invited twenty of their friends and picked a very cool band. We'll do it a week from next Monday when the restaurant is closed. Hon, will you please invite Andre, the Macher, Sara, Alvaro, and, of course, their baby…" She watched him, aware that he wasn't listening, sipping a second drink that Jill had effortlessly set down on the table. She waited, concerned that he was unusually distracted. "Yo, babe, come back to earth. Did you hear a word of what I was explaining?"

He turned to look at her. "Sorry, I'm having trouble concentrating. It's not about you. I'm not sure what's causing it."

"Would you like to talk about it? I'd be happy to listen."

"I don't know what to say."

"That's not like you."

"None of this is like me." His face changed, darker. "And please let it go, you're making me uncomfortable."

"I'm making you uncomfortable? Whoa, babe, it's me you're talking to, the gal who's in love with you."

"Don't make it into a big deal, Callie. Just let it go."

"Are you looking to create a problem between us? If you remember, this happened three days ago. I was asking about Sara, about her baby, and you were short with me, told me you didn't want to talk about her or him."

"So? I didn't want to talk about that, and I don't want to talk about this."

"Listen to yourself. Are you unhappy with me? About anything?"

Cash frowned. "Why can't you just let this alone?"

"Because I'm in love with you, even when you act like a jerk…and something is wrong. And if you can get off your high horse, you'll know that's true."

Cash turned away, took a breath.

"You remember, less than a week ago, you were irritated with the Macher on the phone about some complicated, possibly illegal gem deal. He was concerned, worried about you. He let it go, but he asked me about it later."

Cash turned back.

Callie touched his forearm, tender.

He took her hand, another breath. "Okay, yeah…I'm sorry… You're right…something is off, wrong, and I have no idea what it is."

"What can you tell me about it?"

"Well, I'm depressed often, and that, in turn, makes me quick to anger. More and more, I'm quick to anger, like now, for no reason." He paused, thinking about something.

She waited, patiently.

"Truthfully, lately, I've been preoccupied with my past, even my childhood. Nothing specific, nothing I can focus on... But I'm missing my mother. Remembering things about her. As you know, she died when I was seven. I haven't really thought about her for many years."

"Do you have any idea why this is happening now?"

"It might be because I have a new daughter. But I don't know why that would make me angry."

"What about your grandson? You do have a new three-month-old grandson."

"He, and Sara, are the most exciting things that have happened to me since I fell in love with you. Why—how—could Sara's baby possibly make me angry or get me depressed?"

"That's a good question. Honey, in my opinion, you could use some good help, an expert in sorting out things like this. I know a good man, a psychiatrist, who could help you."

"A psychiatrist...me, a psychiatrist? Are you kidding?"

"Something is wrong, you said it yourself. You don't have any idea what it is. It's making you depressed and angry. This is what psychiatrists are for...it's what they can help with."

"What would I say to a psychiatrist?"

"Whatever you want..."

"Are you sure about this?"

"I think so, yes, at least it's worth a try... The man I'm thinking of is quirky, a little off, but very smart...a thoughtful, imaginative therapist, you'll like him."

"How do you know this guy?"

"After my divorce, when Lew was eleven, and I was working nonstop at the restaurant, he helped Lew. At the time, Lew was having trouble at school. Over a year, he worked it out with him in therapy."

"How come I've never heard of this guy?"

"You're not exactly the type of guy I'd talk to about my son's therapist, though you've seen him." She raised a hand to shush him so she could explain. "About a year ago, soon after we came back from Cuba, he and his wife came to the restaurant. He had me do something special for her birthday. She's a pistol, nothing, and I mean nothing like him. She's younger than he is, and she's tough—fished salmon in Alaska, able to navigate on her own in wild country. She's kind of wild herself and beautiful. He's often preoccupied and distracted, big, with bushy eyebrows, not so good at managing in the world. He has a driver. He admitted that he lost his driver's license because he kept sideswiping cars. No kidding. I remember introducing you to them."

"I do vaguely remember that. They're the ones that didn't quite fit together."

"Yeah, you asked something inappropriate about them after."

"Me? What?"

"First, you asked if I was sure they were together… When I nodded, you asked—in your matter-of-fact way—perhaps they have a great love life? My mouth dropped open, then you actually asked… Could he be giving her unusual sexual favors?"

"I did ask that…"

"You did. At first, I was speechless. I mean, why would you ask something like that?"

"It wasn't meant to be inappropriate. I was speculating, curious about them. This is one unlikely couple—a special sex life, that would be a nice touch. True love."

"You're shameless, but you're not stupid. He's not at all what he looks like. He's, well, unexpected. He could do something like that."

"Right? And you're asking me to see him as my therapist?"

"Yes, I am. That's precisely why I'm asking you to see him. He'll get you, even like you."

"Don't you think I can figure this out without a shrink?"

"Unlikely. You're stuck, lost, more confused, uncertain, than I've ever seen you. It's worrying me. I want you to figure this out. I need you to figure this out. Right away. Okay?"

"Sexual favors?"

"Deal… You won't be disappointed."

CHAPTER ONE

Dr. Abraham Stein's office was near Pioneer Square, an older part of downtown and a tourist destination. Cash liked the old brick buildings, the tired-looking bars, the renovated one-time buck-and-a-quarter hotels, the street life—not so much the tourist shops or the trendy galleries. He found Dr. Stein's brick building under the viaduct. He went through the old wooden door surprised by the busy, well-worn interior. Inside, he saw a luckless-looking pet store, an antique furniture emporium, and this hole-in-the-wall Chinese take-out. Cash took in the smells of Chinese food; he liked this guy already. He saw that Stein's office was on the third floor. He passed the elevator and chose the stairs. On the stairs, he enjoyed hints of sweet and sour pork.

The waiting room was beige, quiet, and comfortable. Several magazines lay on the coffee table. He recognized the *New Yorker*, *Vanity Fair*, *Travel + Leisure*, and wondered who read an old issue of *The Economist* while waiting to see their therapist. Cash sat on a brown corduroy couch. It faced another door. A button-sized light near the inner door was on. The light went off. He recognized the burly guy with bushy salt-and-pepper eyebrows who opened the door and offered a meaty hand.

"Nice to see you again," Abe Stein said.

"Likewise, I hope," Cash replied, looking the doctor over. He guessed Dr. Stein was a little older than him, say fifty-two. He was vaguely off-looking, like he didn't get out much. Cash stood, shook Stein's hand. The doctor's handshake was firm. "Cash Logan," he said.

"Abe Stein," the doctor replied.

Stein didn't care how he looked; Cash could see that right away. His tweed sport coat had a hole in the pocket where something had burned through. His grey wool tie was loose at the collar and hung askew. He showed a large palm, ushering Cash into his office.

The office was a lived-in, cozy room with an oversized dark oak table and two chairs near the far window. On the near side of the table there was an old, worn red leather chair. On the far side there was a contemporary high-backed desk chair. Papers were in piles on the table, held down with blackened pipes, pipe racks, and ashtrays. Two open cans of Diet Coke sat on Dr. Stein's side of the phone. Beyond the table, wooden blinds covered the windows. On the wall behind him, Cash had seen two dissimilar paintings. One was colorful, modern. The other was a black-and-white portrait of a bearded man with glasses in a black suit. Stein motioned for Cash to sit, then sat on his own high-back desk chair. He spoke softly, carefully, "Please, tell me how I can help."

"I'm new to this, so please bear with me. Truthfully, I don't know the answer to your question. I'm not at all sure you can help."

"Try me… Take your time."

Cash nodded, thoughtful, then shrugged unsure what to say.

Abe suggested, "What would you ask me to do if you thought I could help?"

Smart. Give him a chance. "There's one thing. Lately, I get low, then get headaches, and I'm quick to anger. And there's no reason for it that I understand. This is new for me. Inexplicable. I've always been very level-headed, slow to anger. I'd like to go back to what I've always been. Can you help me with something like this?"

"Maybe. Anything else you'd ask for if you thought I could help?"

"You make this like a game for children—'pretend I'm a genie, what would you ask for?'"

"That will work too, though I assure you, I'm no genie. But if I were, and if you had another wish, what would you ask me for?"

Cash looked him in the eye. "First, what would you like me to call you? Dr. Stein?"

"If you'd like, but I'm fine if you call me Abe."

"I'll call you Abe then."

"Good. What shall I call you?"

"Cash. Call me Cash."

"Fair enough. Anything else, Cash, you'd ask for if you thought I could help?"

Smart and tenacious. "Okay, Genie. This is right up your alley. Recently, I've been preoccupied with my past, even my childhood. Nothing specific, nothing I can focus on… But I'm missing my mother. Remembering things about her. She died when I was seven… I haven't really thought about her for many years. Maybe four months ago, not long before my grandson was born, I started thinking a lot about her again, dreaming about her. And I don't want to hear any psychobabble about dreaming about my mother."

"You're tough. Tell me about your grandson."

"This is a long story. It begins almost two years ago. A young woman I'd never met found us at Callie's restaurant. She was half-Algerian, twenty-five years old. Her name was Sara. She told us a shocking, unbelievable story. Someone was trying to kill her, and they'd stolen her identity. She carefully told us her stunning, life-changing story, and then, at the end, she explained and provided convincing proof that she was my daughter. We even had blood tests. In the next several months, we saved her life and got her identity back. Along the way, she fell in love with a fine Cuban young man. Her son, they call him Young Cash, or Baby Cash, is my grandson."

"Well, Cash, we have work to do, but if you agree, I'd like to try and help you."

"How long is this work likely to take?"

"There's no way to predict that. It could be six months or a year until we even know what we're hoping to understand, to sort out, and why."

"That's too long. I'll work hard. I'll come often. I'll follow your lead, go down whatever dark, frightening hole you want to lead me into, but I want to know that this can happen sooner."

"How often are you willing to come?"

"Once a week, even twice a week."

"If you come more often, three or even four times a week, we may—I repeat MAY—at least understand why this is happening sooner. No guarantees."

"I see that my genie has limitations."

"Sadly, that's true. The kind of things you want to explore, to understand, will take time to ferret out, to unravel, and then time to know what they actually mean to you, why they mean that. That said, this is worth working on, figuring out, and I think you'll be good at it, at least unafraid of it." He took a pipe from his desk. Even the outside of the bowl was charred. "Do you mind?" he asked.

"Isn't there a no-smoking ordinance?" Cash asked.

Abe cracked the window behind him. "Yes, but my landlord is in China. If it bothers you, I won't smoke."

"I'm okay with it."

Abe struck a wooden match. He held the match over the bowl and inhaled until smoke began to plume. When he was satisfied, he dropped the match into an ashtray beside him. He went on, "How do you feel about coming more often? It's a big commitment. If you like working with me, though, it is, I think, our best chance at succeeding timely… Of course, if it doesn't work for you, we can change it."

Cash was watching the match, still burning near a pile of papers where it had landed, when it slid from the ashtray.

"Is something wrong?" Abe asked, when Cash didn't respond. He was watching Cash, intent. His brow was furrowed, and his eyebrows almost touched like a "V."

Maybe it was the expression on Cash's face, or perhaps he smelled smoke. Whatever it was, Abe Stein finally turned to see that his papers had just caught fire. He picked up a can of Diet Coke and doused the flame, like it was no big deal. A little pool of Diet Coke puddled on his desk.

"This happen often?"

"More than I like to admit."

"Your landlord know about this?"

"He lives in Hong Kong."

"I see."

"I'm absent-minded," Abe explained. "Not a good quality for a pipe smoker."

"You got a fire extinguisher?"

"I prefer Diet Coke."

Cash looked at the doctor, possibly his doctor. Abe's eyes were pale blue, and they were smart eyes. Cash took a careful, measured breath, exhaled slowly. "I'll come four times a week."

Abe shook his hand. "Tomorrow, eleven a.m.?"

Cash stuck up his thumb.

"Bring your calendar; we'll work out a regular schedule tomorrow."

"Truthfully, I can't believe I agreed to do this."

"Let's try it."

◆◆◆

Cash was sitting at the long maple prep table in the kitchen at the restaurant. He was drinking a latte with rich, foamy cream that Callie had prepared the way he liked it. She sat kitty-corner from him, drinking her own cappuccino with skim milk.

Cash touched her forearm and said, "I agreed to see him four times a week."

"You what? Four times a week? No…you're kidding? That's not therapy; it's psychoanalysis."

"What's that?"

"That's four times a week, and sometimes you lay back on a couch and the analyst sits behind you, so you can't see him or her."

"No, he didn't suggest anything like that…no, nothing."

"How'd you get to four times a week then?"

"Well, he was saying it might take six months or a year before we even knew what we were looking for. So I said, let's speed it up."

"Well, that sounds like you—when you do something, you really do it. You must have liked him."

"I did like him. He's like you said—very smart, not rigid, in fact, willing to do things in unusual ways. I don't think he would have encouraged me if he didn't think we could succeed. Truthfully, for the first time in a long while, he made me feel hopeful."

"Say more about that."

"He said he thought that I'd be good at this, that he sensed that I wasn't afraid to look at dark, difficult things. I have no idea how he knew that."

"He's right about you…and that's fast…and he wouldn't say these things if he didn't mean them… It sounds like a good start."

"Maybe… So you know what I did? During all of this, with no experience at all, I decided—I actually figured this out, got this idea, right there in his office—that for this to work, I had to throw away the rules, be willing to say things I wouldn't normally say. Take risks. Find out right away if he could step up, if he was the real deal."

"Oh, Cash, you didn't?"

"Didn't what?"

"You know exactly what. You asked him, didn't you?"

"Not exactly."

"Jesus, Cash, you're a menace, a relentless troublemaker. You actually asked your therapist if he gave his wife unusual sexual favors—"

"Honey, not to worry. I'm joking. This was my first therapy joke."

"It wasn't remotely funny…and you are out of control, hopeless."

Cash raised her up, put his arms around her waist.

Her face was red, a bad sign.

"I'm doing this therapy, right?"

She frowned.

"For you, but for me, too."

Cash kissed her, tenderly. She resisted, though she didn't move away.

She backed away from him, relenting. "You're still a hopeless, troublemaker…but I love you very much."

◆◆◆

Cash was wandering through the Pike Place Market. He'd picked up some fresh king salmon for Césaire, Callie's chef, who was creating a new bouillabaisse dish on the menu tonight. He'd stopped to pay homage to the Pike Market piggy bank, Rachel, the bronze pig. Callie had named her restaurant, Le Cochon Bronze, after Rachel, and Cash liked to put a few dollars in whenever he went by. Next, he took a digression down Post Alley to see the Gum Wall. Cash wasn't sure why, but he often came by to check out the long brick wall, covered in used chewing gum, south of the market's main entrance off First Street. The wall was fifteen feet high along a fifty-foot-long section, and the gum coating alongside the wall was several inches thick. Cash knew that in 2015, all of the gum on the wall was removed (2,350 pounds of gum), and the wall underneath had been steam cleaned. A new layer of gum appeared quickly, added by visitors and local residents immediately after the cleanup. It took approximately five months to bring it back to its original colorful look. Though he couldn't explain why, the gum wall was one of the unexpected things that Cash liked about Seattle. This quirky, unique attraction has become one of the city's most popular destinations, particularly enjoyed by children. It was, Cash thought, the kind of distinctive Seattle eccentric sensibility that would be rejected in New York or San Francisco or Houston as being a gross, germ-infested monstrosity, whereas in Seattle, many saw the Gum Wall as a work of collective art, an example of Seattle's charm and character.

He meandered on, up to First and north toward Le Pichet, where he was meeting his friend, Detective Ed Samter, for lunch. At the busy intersection at Pine, Cash noticed an older man across from him, on the far corner. The man wore a faded basketball cap. Cash recognized the vintage green and red Seattle Supersonics hat. It had a red brim, and on the green top of the hat stood the old orange, red, and green Sonics emblem. In the middle of the emblem, the Seattle Space Needle rose in white. Cash felt an unexpected sad tinge seeing the familiar hat. He'd owned the same hat years ago, when, as a kid, he followed the young Sonics team. He was still upset that the Sonics left in 2008 to go to

Oklahoma. He still blamed Howard Schultz, the founder of Starbucks, who led a group that acquired the Sonics in 2001 and foolishly sold the team to the group that ended up moving them to Oklahoma City. Cash felt a flash of anger, surprised that this could still bother him. Then, he reminded himself that these days it didn't take much to get him irritated.

He looked left, down toward the Market and the water beyond. Taking a diversion down that street, he saw one of his favorite hotels, Inn at the Market, just below him on Pine Street. He stopped to walk down and look beyond the hotel through the window at a café he liked, Café Campagne. It was a reliable fine meal with the same pleasant ambiance since 1994, and then he was back up the hill and around the corner at his destination, Le Pichet, on his left on First. Inside, he saw Ed Samter sipping red wine at the table facing a front window. Le Pichet was small, unpretentious, an authentic bistro specializing in classic regional cuisine—charcuterie, Confit de Canard, Poulet Roti, and so on. Inside, there was a narrow, small space with a few tables, banquets, tables and chairs along the wall, tiles on the floor, an unassuming marble bar on the opposite wall, and an old barrel sitting in the middle with various sample treats and alcohols sitting on top. You'd never understand what a special, carefully thought-out bistro it was, unless you took the time to get to know it.

Samter stood to shake hands with his friend. "Too long," he said, as Cash shook his hand, then looked around the simple bistro.

"Good to see you, Ed." Cash smiled, then sat down opposite the tall, fit, quiet detective. He and Ed had been through a lot, and he'd grown very fond of him.

"How have you been?" Ed asked.

"Truthfully, I've been kind of low. Depressed, I think. I don't know why I'm telling you this, except you're a good friend."

"You getting any help with that?"

"I started working with a psychiatrist that Callie recommended. Guy named Abe Stein."

"You're in excellent hands. I know him. He's great."

"How do you know him? You ever work with him?"

"No, but he's friends with a good friend of mine, Lieutenant Ballard, and people in the department know about him. In his way, he's a character, a little bit of a favorite story. It's complicated."

"Even better. I'm hoping to learn about him. Please tell me what you can."

"Sure. His mom is Jesse Stein, the political kingmaker. She was an item with Nick Season, maybe twelve years ago. You remember him?"

"The guy was a big-shot lawyer. He was running for State Attorney General, right?"

"Yeah, Jesse Stein was his lover and his campaign manager—"

"Oh Jesus, it's coming back. That's the guy who got killed, shot on some sandspit in the middle of nowhere. I remember that."

"That's the guy. The man that killed him, shot him in the chest, twice, that was your therapist, Abe Stein."

"Go on! That's impossible. Are you making this up? No way!"

"Listen carefully, Abe Stein is not at all what he seems. Lou Ballard knows him pretty well, swears by him. He told me the whole story, and Lou is hard to impress. You want the details?"

"Absolutely. Everything."

"Well, so here's what happened. Corey, the woman behind all of this, was in prison, framed. When she got out, all she wanted was to get her son back from foster care. She went to see Abe Stein for an evaluation for the dependency court. She needed Abe to tell the court that she was a "fit parent." After going back and forth, sorting out a few missteps, Abe agreed to do that. He liked her. She wasn't in therapy, not a patient, and by now, he liked her a lot more than an evaluee. Long story short, he asked her to come to brunch at one of his mother's regular Sunday events. She came. Who was there—Nick Season, Abe's mother's boyfriend, the same man that framed Corey. He saw her, and the rest is history."

"Oh God."

"It was a disaster. Corey took off with her son on her boat, up the Inside Passage. Abe was beside himself, and he decided to go after her.

My friend Lou helped Abe find Corey. Now, as you can imagine, Abe couldn't swim. Nevertheless, Abe jumped out of a float plane, wearing this oversized life jacket, in front of Corey's old hardtop Chris Craft wooden boat. By now, Abe knows that his mother's candidate and lover is going to try and kill Corey. Against all odds, Abe convinces Corey to come back and take on Nick Season, the front-runner for the new State Attorney General. Now Corey was tough, and she knew how dangerous Nick was. The fact that Abe convinced her to come back, convinced her that together they could stop Nick Season, gives you a taste of who Abe Stein really is. This is a long, complicated story, so I'll cut to the chase."

"Take your time. I'm hooked."

"Well, I get that, it's a showstopper…okay…so Abe sets up a meeting through his mother with Nick Season on this remote sandspit off an island among Canada's Gulf Islands. They'd meet by boat. After securing his boat, then coming onto the sandspit, without warning, Nick took charge. He sat next to Abe on a log, then pulled out a hidden icepick and stuck it into Abe's ear. After showing Corey the icepick in Abe's ear, he forced her to throw her gun into the ocean. Next, Nick took out his own gun, made Abe stand, facing away toward the water, then throw his gun away. Roughly, he flung Corey face-down on the sand. After cuffing Corey's hand behind her back, Nick viciously pistol-whipped Abe's head and face until he, too, lay on the sand beyond the log, covering his bloody face in his arms. Nick kicked Abe savagely, several times, then pulled Corey's hair, raising her up, standing, with his ice pick in her lower jaw. Corey screamed until Nick pulled out the pick and let her drop to the sand. Nick called Abe, lying battered behind the log. 'Come on over here, Sir Lancelot,' Nick said. 'We're going boating.' Nick turned toward Abe, gesturing with his gun for Abe to move along, then turned toward the water. In that instant, Abe brought his right hand up from behind the log with a handgun in it. A gun he'd hidden behind the log a day earlier without telling anyone.

"Nick must have sensed something. When he spun back toward Abe, his gun raised, Abe fired two shots. Two in the chest. Centered."

Cash just starred at Ed Samter. Cash's eyes were bulging, his mouth open wide.

Samter smiled. "People still talk about what Abe said to Nick Season as he died…and what Corey said, after."

"Please tell me." Cash almost whispered, plainly dumbstruck.

"Nick looked up from his back lying on the sand. 'You?' he sputtered, uncomprehending.

"Abe took a breath. 'I get it about you, Nick. Think about that. How could I possibly understand you and still be anything like I'm supposed to be?'

"That was the last thing Nick heard before he died.

"Then Corey lay her head on Abe's shoulder, saying softly, 'The shrink who can't drive put Nick Season down like a rabid dog. It takes my breath away.'"

Cash reached over, briefly tapped Ed Samter's forearm. "That's an unbelievable story. I had no idea."

"Corey and Abe were married soon after. To hear Lou Ballard tell it, they're still wildly in love."

"I wouldn't have guessed something like that in a thousand years."

"No one ever does. I've seen Abe Stein crack some very tough cases when the cops working on them were spinning their wheels, lost without a clue."

"Corey was right. He's not at all—nothing—like what he looks like, or as he said to Nick Season, 'anything like what I'm supposed to be…' You're making me feel better."

"You and Abe Stein, you're gonna do just fine—two peas in a pod. Let's order, I'm hungry—Rillettes de pork, Assiette de charcuterie, Gratin Lyonnais. What else suits your fancy?"

"It's on you. Show off your fancy French. Go wild. I'm paying."

◆◆◆

When Cash came back to The Bronze Pig, it was already 3:30. He went through the back door into the kitchen and was delighted to see his daughter, Sara, her husband, Alvaro, and their three-and-a-half month son, Baby Cash, asleep in Sara's arms. They were all seated around the maple prep table, drinking cappuccino. Callie was behind the table putting together cookies and pastries.

Cash put his arm around Sara, kissed the sleeping baby gently, and placed his free hand on Alvaro's shoulder. "What a nice surprise," he said. He stepped back to take Callie's hand, after she set down the sweets. "I saw Ed, and do I have a story about Abe Stein."

"I can't wait."

"Who's Abe Stein?" Sara asked, not wanting to miss a thing.

Callie looked at Cash, a question.

Cash nodded.

Callie turned to Sara, "Your dad is in therapy. Abe Stein is his therapist."

Sara smiled wide. "Okay…wow. That's great news."

"Why?" Cash asked.

"We were worried about you."

"You were…about what?"

"I'm sure you're aware that you've been getting angry easily. Inappropriately. And you do seem depressed."

"I didn't think you knew about that?"

"I'm your daughter, Dad. I think about you, and when you're not doing well, I worry about you."

Callie smiled, put her hand on Sara's shoulder.

"Like what?"

"Like last week when you went off on Alvaro about spending too much time on his Florida business, about how he should be spending more time with his new family."

"Well, he should, damnit." Cash responded, irritated. "Hell, do I need to explain that again?"

"That's exactly what I mean. Our family is great. Alvaro never does anything before we both agree. Same for me. And not only are you simply wrong about this, it's way out of line to talk about it in this way."

Callie jumped in, "She's right. It's what we've been talking about."

Cash sighed, put a palm up. "Okay…okay."

The baby was waking up, aroused by the tense interchange. Sara stood, handed Young Cash, who was crying now, to Callie.

Cash looked at the startled baby. "Sorry. If both of you agree, and apparently, the baby agrees too, I'm sure you're right. Alvaro, does that include you?" Cash turned.

"Yes, if it wasn't so obviously out of character, I would have responded angrily last time. Instead, we tried to figure out what was going on. What might be wrong? We even asked Callie about it earlier today, and she said that no one, including you, seemed to know. Can you help?"

"No. Not really. That's why, thanks to a strong push from Callie, I went into therapy. And since everyone seems to be more aware of this than I knew, I can only ask all of you to bear with me. I can promise you that I can't imagine four other people—I'm including my spectacular grandson—that I love and respect more. So, if I'm being unfairly angry, I sincerely apologize for what I've done. I wish I could say that it won't happen again, but I can't. I have no idea why this is happening, and I'm afraid it will happen again. I'm worried that I may inadvertently make a mistake, do something stupid, hurt a loved one. This is all totally new for me. And very hard for me to control or manage. That's why I need help. Good help."

"Say more," Sara asked.

"It's like there's something going on inside of me that I don't understand. I think it's trying to get out, to surface, but I can't quite reach it—that's my best guess about where the anger is coming from. It's too early to tell, but I think I may have a good therapist, and I'm hoping he'll help."

"Let us help, however we can," Sara said.

"As you know, we'll all do that," Callie added, as Sara passed the cookies and pastries. "Now. Tell me about Abe Stein. That has to be good." Callie rocked the baby, easily.

Cash smiled at his grandson, then at Callie, who had fixed her eyes on him, waiting eagerly. "Short version. I was asking the wrong question." Cash nodded, pausing, adding fuel to her eagerness. "The question is not—does he give his wife unusual sexual favors?"

Sara made a face, "Dad, no?"

"Don't worry, I didn't ask that… The question is—would he kill his own mother's lover, to give Corey the opportunity to become his wife?"

"No. No…Abe Stein?" Callie asked, a tense whisper.

"He did that… His mother's lover was Nick Season, the front-runner for State Attorney General, the same man who framed Abe's wife-to-be, Corey. Abe convinced Corey to come back and face Nick rather than run away. He convinced her to face him together. Abe lured Nick in, then when Nick tried to kill them both, Abe, the shrink who couldn't drive, shot Nick twice in the chest."

"Your therapist did that?" Sara asked, breathless.

"He did."

"I never heard of a shrink like that… Hire that guy."

"That's pretty much what Callie told me to do."

Callie passed the baby to Cash, then took Cash's arm. "So now, maybe you'll listen to what I say?"

"I am trying, babe, believe me."

Cash held the baby gently, tenderly. He rocked him slowly as he walked around the table. The baby made happy little cooing sounds, relaxing.

"You're wonderful with him," Alvaro noted.

"That's true." Sara nodded. "Please don't worry about hurting us with your inexplicable anger," Sara implored. "After what you've said, we'll be pretty thick-skinned."

"That would be good. I have a favor, and it's serious. I want you all to keep an eye on me. This is real. Most importantly, please don't leave me alone with Young Cash." He cradled his grandson. "I had a dream where I was carrying him, and I dropped him without even knowing why. That scared me a lot."

"You don't need to worry about that, Dad," Sara said, in her unmistakable certain way. "I'll make sure that that never happens."

Cash gently gave the baby back to Sara. "Thank you for that. It helps me."

"When you see Abe tomorrow, ask him what we can do specifically to help," Callie said. "I think this has just now become all of our problem, which is what it should have been earlier. There's something scaring you, Cash. Yes, some of it is hidden in memories, but let's not treat it as just a psychological disorder. There has to be a reason—real or imagined or both. We don't have to decide that now. My bet, hell, my certainty, is that whatever is scaring you has a real component. Let's treat it the same way we dealt with Sara being in danger, or me and my restaurant at risk. You and Abe will have to figure out what's going on, but let us work with you as you do. As you've taught us, we're all best when we work together on this kind of inexplicable, thorny problem. I know you. There's more bothering you than some forgotten childhood memory or fantasy. If there's something to worry about, let's be ready."

"You're ahead of me, which I appreciate. Something is scaring me. If it's real, we need to address it. I'll talk with Abe about this tomorrow."

◆◆◆

Cash was already standing when Abe opened the door from his office to the waiting room. He started right in when they were seated at Abe's desk. "I have a lot to talk about. Is it okay for me to begin?"

"Of course."

"Two different subjects. One, I learned about you, Corey, and Nick Season. Chapeau..." Cash tipped an imaginary hat to Abe, who smiled. "But it raises many other questions I'd like to ask. The second subject is about me. I spent a long time talking with Callie and my daughter and her husband, while playing with my grandson. By the end of those conversations, we all seemed to think that, though I don't know what it is, there is possibly something real that I am frightened about related to, but not necessarily the same as whatever repressed memory I am trying to find. Both are important subjects, but I'm guessing you'd like to start with what I'm thinking about myself. Is that right?"

"Not necessarily. First, it doesn't surprise me that you've gone so far so quickly. This kind of intensity, and purpose, is what I sensed about you. So the answer to your question is that this is up to you. I will happily talk with you about my history with Nick Season. Or we can begin learning more about you."

"Let's start with me then. If we can get a jump start on that, that would be helpful. Before we start, I will say that what I learned about you and Nick Season was impressive and unexpected. You're an uncommon man."

"Thank you. I appreciate that."

"Okay. I can't stop thinking about what is working on me, what I can't quite reach. I have one clue that may be a starting place. I had a dream last night; it's actually a similar dream to one I've had before. In this dream, I'm carrying my grandson, trying to put him to sleep. I get distracted. In the dream, it's because my long-dead mother comes into the room, and I drop the baby, inadvertently. He falls on his head on the hard floor. He doesn't die, but his head is badly hurt. When I pick him up, my mother is gone. Yesterday, I told my daughter, her husband, and Callie that I wanted them to be sure that they never leave me alone with the baby, that I was afraid of dropping him, hurting him by mistake. They agreed to help me with that. But I'm not at all sure what the dream means."

"First off, you were smart to ask them to keep an eye on you. It will give you a level of protection that should be comforting. To understand what it means, I need to learn more about your family, about your life growing up. Are you comfortable talking to me about that?"

"I, frankly, don't remember very much about it, but I'll tell you what I do remember."

"Start wherever you'd like."

"My mother and father died in a car crash when I was seven. I don't really remember the details, but the car went over a steep cliff, on fire, onto the rocks in the water below. Years later, I read the police report. Her boss from the port identified my mother, and two reliable witnesses, including his cousin, identified my father. The coroner and the policemen in charge confirmed that my father had been drinking heavily, drunk, they said. There was a high level of alcohol in his blood, more than 0.20 percent. The police and the coroner concluded that his drunken driving had caused the accident. I was sent to my mother's parents, who raised me until they died—my grandfather died when I was sixteen. My grandmother died when I was eighteen. That's when I went into the army."

"What were your mother and father like? Do you remember your time with them as a child?"

"I remember my mother as warm and present and always responsive. She was what I remember most about my early years. My father was unpredictable, and I didn't see him much. He came home late, and I was usually asleep. I do remember that he could get very angry—scary—especially when he was drinking. He hit me once, and I ran away to hide. I spent the night in the shed."

"Did he hit you often?"

"Not that I remember."

"Did your father have any relatives—parents, brothers and sisters, cousins—that you ever met?"

"None that I knew of?"

"Did he ever talk about any relatives?"

"My mom once said he had a cousin in Canada, but we never knew him."

"Did your father ever mention him?"

"Not that I remember."

"But you did keep in touch with your mother's parents, even before she died?"

"Yes."

"What were your grandparents like?"

"Very nice. A lot like my mom. They were available, and we talked a lot after my mother died, as I was growing up. I had a good life with them. I do remember those years, especially as I became a teenager, and those are good memories."

"Did you talk often with your grandparents about your mom and dad?"

"At first, just to let me move on. Then, when I was a little older, I had lots of questions about what actually happened, how it happened. They helped me work with the police to answer my questions. The police seemed to understand the accident. They were thorough and helpful. My grandparents even got my parents' medical records for me to keep in case my own doctor ever needed them."

"Were you satisfied with what you learned?"

"At the time, yes—the police even explained the details, including the fire—but I was fourteen years old. After that, we stopped talking about it. It was still a sad subject for all of us."

"Why do you think you're worried about hurting your grandson?"

"I don't know."

"Why do you think your mother is in the dream?"

"I don't know."

"Is it possible that she wants to tell you something?

"It's possible. I think she was starting to say something when I dropped the baby."

"Do you have any idea what it might be?"

"No, not really."

"Could it be a warning?"

"Why would you think that?"

"Well, she died unexpectedly."

"What if she's trying to tell me how to protect my grandson?"

"She could be. Is it possible that there's something about her death that you don't know?"

"The police report was pretty thorough, but I was young and parts of it were hard to understand. So yes, of course, I should go back and look at that again."

"It can't hurt."

"I have a couple of close friends who've worked with me often. They're skilled—professional smugglers, diamond traders, experts at working outside the system. Yesterday, Callie said, and I'll try to quote this, 'My bet, hell, my certainty, is that whatever is scaring you has a real component. Let's treat it the same way we dealt with Sara being in danger, or me and my restaurant at risk. You and Abe will have to figure out what's going on but let us work with you as you do.' I'd like to put one man from this team on finding out exactly what happened to my parents. If there's anything to find, he'll discover it."

"It's unconventional, but like you, it's smart. If we want to move quickly, let's put your skilled experts on it. It won't slow down our work, and it could help."

"I'll get him on it today. I understand that this is unconventional, but he'll be discrete—no one will know what he's up to."

"Good. Now, can you tell me more about your mom and dad?"

"I've been thinking, remembering things, about my mom lately. I think it's because I have a daughter, and she's just become a mom."

"That's possible… What are you remembering?"

"Little things—how she liked to sing to me, read to me, play games with me, and talk with me."

"Those seem like good, happy memories."

"They are."

"Are there any others?"

"Once, I went in to see her, and she didn't want to play. She looked like she might have been crying."

"Do you remember anything else about that time with her?"

"No, whenever I try to find more, I lose the memory entirely. It's hard to explain; it's like it just vanishes."

"That's not uncommon with difficult memories. Give us a little time; we'll learn how to find more."

"How can we do that?"

"It's not a special technique or an abstract idea. What we'll do is discuss other memories, think about other things, follow your mind in other directions. I'll ask you about other related thoughts. We'll see what happens, play it by ear, and you may be pleasantly surprised."

"And I'm paying for that plan? Are you kidding? Never mind. How long will that take?"

"It could happen in weeks or in months, or never."

"Great. This is like hoping to win the lottery?"

"No, it's not about drawing a random number. It's about allowing yourself to access, to feel, difficult, unwelcome things. It takes work; it often takes courage. Some people are never able to do it. I'm even more certain than ever that you'll be able to do it sooner than most."

"What can I do to help with that?"

"Do what you're doing, but take the pressure off. You can't force it. You can't do exercises or train for it. The best thing you can do is to stop blaming yourself, try to forgive yourself for bad things that you've done or imagined that you've done, accept unwanted thoughts or unthinkable fantasies. In this interior, often unconscious world, harsh judgments, blame, or remorse can be obstacles. I'd never say this to some people, but in your case, I'm comfortable recommending that you simply let yourself off the hook. Focus on your wonderful friends, your lovely partner, your new daughter, grandson, and son-in-law."

"That sounds awfully good. I'm not sure I can do that, though. In my work, when I'm trading diamonds, or rugs, or even Japanese ivory carvings, Netsuke, I'm always worrying about what can go wrong, what I may have missed, who can trick me or cheat me. When something goes wrong, I'm usually right to blame myself."

"In this world, especially in this room, take a break from all of that. There's no one except you inside your mind. Try to go easy on yourself, be more accepting than you might normally be."

"You mean there are harsh judgments, things that I blame myself for, that get in my way, that keep me from accessing my own memories."

"Something like that, sometimes."

"I'm not sure what you're asking me to do. I don't even know what to stop blaming myself for. I have no list of what, as a kid, I may have done wrong."

"You may not even have done it. You may just think you did or convince yourself that you must have done it."

"How would that work?"

"Both of your parents died in a car crash when you were very young. A seven-year-old child won't understand why that happened to him. It's a horrible, unbearable punishment; why did it happen to you?"

"Because I wasn't a good enough son?"

"Of course not, but a seven-year-old might fear that such an unthinkable event would never have happened otherwise. If only you'd loved your father more, if only you'd idealized him as he wanted you to—"

"Or if I didn't really, secretly, want to hurt him."

"Did you?"

"I did wish that he was not so angry...that he was nicer to me and took better care of my mother."

"Can you say more?"

"Like what?" Cash put two fingers on his right temple, massaging a headache that was coming on.

"Like how he could have taken better care of your mother."

"Why do you keep asking me that?"

"Because you said it."

"Can you just back off and stop putting words in my mouth?"

"Do you think I'm doing that?"

"Obviously. I know what you want me to say, want me to think, and I'm getting tired of how you try to get me to say things I may not want to say." He was rubbing his neck now with one hand while he pressed his right temple with two fingers.

"Do you have a headache? Are you angry?"

"Yes...yes."

"Why?"

"You're being a jerk."

"How?"

"Just back off."

"Okay. Let's carry on tomorrow."

"If I come…"

"That's up to you. But please, give us a chance to figure out why you get so irrationally angry. I think I've just had a glimpse of it, and you need to learn to manage it."

"Fuck you."

"Hope to see you tomorrow."

Cash stood, turned to the door, and then he turned back. "This was a mistake."

"Think about it. Sleep on it, before you decide."

◆◆◆

When Cash got back to the restaurant, Sara was still there, breastfeeding Baby Cash. Both she and Callie were sitting at the long maple prep table in the kitchen. Cash kissed each of them and then the baby.

After a moment, Callie asked, "I know it's private, but is it alright if I ask how it went with your therapist?"

"It's okay to ask today, anyway, because I'd like to talk about it."

"Good. I'm, of course, very interested in how the two of you are doing."

"Not so good. I got really angry with him this morning."

Callie winced. "Did you have a good reason?"

"I thought so. I mean, he kept asking me questions that I didn't like, that pointed me in a direction I didn't want to go."

"So you blasted him."

"More or less."

Sara looked at her dad. "I'm no expert, but that should be okay with your therapist. It is, after all, why you're there."

Callie nodded. "If you let him explore it, it may help you understand why it happens."

"When he explores private things that I don't want to talk about, it just gives me a headache and makes me angry. I can't seem to control it."

"You don't have to. He's good. Now, he's seen it happen. Let him pursue it. You can get as angry as you want."

"I told him seeing him was a mistake…I may quit."

"Please don't do that."

"Why?"

"We've been over this. You need help…and it seems to me that these episodes are happening more frequently and lasting longer. You may be mad at him today, but I believe that Abe can help you. When you calm down, even if it takes all day, you'll see that. Please don't do anything you'll regret. For now, stay with him, for me."

"Damnit. Why am I still so angry?"

"It's like being sick. It's out of your control. Don't make a mistake when you're feeling bad."

"At least until tomorrow, for you, I'll stay with it, see where it goes…"

"That's smart," Sara said, relieved.

Cash took a slow breath, changing gears. "In the meantime, he wants me to look into the accident that killed my parents. I took your advice, babe. I called Andre. I put him on it. It happened over forty years ago, outside Tacoma, but if anyone can, Andre can get us started. He's on his way to Tacoma now. He'll come over tonight."

◆◆◆

The older man wore a timeworn leather jacket and a vintage green and red Seattle Supersonics cap. He walked into Grand Central Station, then down the ramp to the lower level. There he sat at one of the open cafes in the center. He ordered coffee and a Danish, then put his cap on the table and waited. He was tall, at least six feet, and he had fine-looking white hair that just about reached his shoulder. He was more than seventy, maybe seventy-four, but still good-looking, with sharp blue eyes. His eyes covered the large downstairs seating areas, taking it all in easily. Not five minutes later, a younger African-American man sat beside him. He was about fifty, sharply dressed in a suit with crew-cut hair. They shook hands, some kind of learned handshake, and smiled.

"Long time, Kit," the younger man said.

"Too long, Gus," Kit, the older man, replied. "You're out how long?"

"Seven months, twenty-three days. You?"

"Twenty-eight days."

"How long were you inside?"

Kit nodded; he knew this. "Ten years, nine months."

"Changed a lot outside. I'm still getting used to it."

"I can't. It just feels off—worn out, shabby, like a used-up whore's puss-dripping pussy." Kit scowled.

"My man, the silver-tongued devil."

Kit smirked. "One thing's the same: money talks."

"That's a fact, boss. I'm ready to talk about that."

"Did you do everything we agreed?"

"Yes, it took time to confirm the details, but basically, my research confirmed the connection, and our initial notion was spot-on."

"Hit me, son."

"Our man, Itzac, is a big shot, a well-known diamond trader. He has easily over one hundred million dollars. He can make the ransom, no sweat."

"We'll ask for fifteen million. We'll split two ways, after we repay our Hong Kong partner. He gets seven, then we'll split eight. Same as we planned."

"What does our Hong Kong partner say?"

"Mr. Chen expects to be paid, promptly."

"When do we go?"

"Two weeks. That work for you?"

"Yes."

"Is Seattle set?"

"It is."

"Let's walk through the specifics."

"Good." Gus smiled. "We worked hard on this, really hard. Mr. Chen should be satisfied."

Kit frowned, suddenly angry. "He's an untrusting, unforgiving, ruthless man. We lost his money. He won't be satisfied until he's paid."

"Can we negotiate him down?"

"Don't even think about it. He's simply the most dangerous man I ever met."

"I'm not worried."

"Why's that?"

"The guy I'm working with, my partner, Kit, right here, he's the most dangerous man I ever met." Gus nodded, giving Kit a thumbs-up.

Kit turned serious. "Listen carefully. The tough guys in prison that tried to muscle us, that wasn't easy, but it never scared me, and we handled it." He nodded, remembering, then changed his tone, a warning. "Mr. Chen, he scares me…and he should scare you, too."

◆◆◆

Cash looked away when he entered Abe's office. He sat down in the worn, comfortable leather chair, looked up, and simply said, "I'm sorry."

"Are you talking about getting angry at me yesterday?"

"I am. It's what keeps happening to me. I get really angry, unnecessarily, then sometime after, I don't understand why."

"There's no need to apologize to me. This is why you're here. Now that I've seen it, let's figure out what happened."

"I can't seem to do that, but I'll help however I can."

"Okay. I was asking you why you wanted to hurt your father."

"I did say that, didn't I?"

"You did."

"I don't remember it very clearly. What exactly did I say?"

"I was wondering if you blamed yourself for your parent's accident. I asked, 'If only you'd loved your father more, if only you'd idealized him as he wanted you to—' Then you interrupted and suggested, 'Or if I didn't really, secretly, want to hurt him.' And I asked, 'Did you?' And you replied, 'I did wish he was not so angry, nicer to me, and took better care of my mother.' Then I asked, 'Can you say more?' And you asked, 'Like what?' and I said, 'Like how he could have taken better care of your mother.' You asked, 'Why do you keep asking me that?' I replied, 'Because you said it.' Then you got angry and said, 'Can you just back off and stop putting words in my mouth?' Do you remember that?"

"When I hear you say it now, I remember some of it. I do remember getting a headache. It's hard to remember things after that. But yes, from what I do remember, what you said sounds right."

"What upset you? What made you so angry?"

Cash took a breath. "I didn't want you to know about it..." Another pause. "As a child, it was—well—my unbearable secret...I didn't want anyone, anyone, to ever know that I wanted to hurt my father. I was sure that it would have had unforgivable...terrible...consequences. In my mind, as a seven-year-old, it did, in fact, have those horrible consequences."

"Yes, that's why you suppressed it. As a child, you could have thought you were responsible for your parent's death. If only you hadn't wanted to hurt your dad, this never would have happened. Now, tell me, why did you want to hurt your father?"

"...not your business."

"It's happening again, isn't it?"

"Yes..."

"Take your time. When you're ready, please try to answer this—Why did you want to hurt your father?"

"Please give me a minute."

Cash stood, rubbed the back of his neck, walked around the room. When he came back to the desk, his face was red, and he was frowning. "It's hard for me to even say it, but...I think...I think he really hurt my mother."

"Is that what you couldn't remember when you saw your mother crying?"

"This is starting to come back. She was hiding her face; she didn't want me to see that her face was bruised…there was another bruise on her shoulder that snaked back under her sleeveless dress." Cash stood again, took a handkerchief out of his pocket, blew his nose, and wiped his eyes. "I remember them fighting. I don't know exactly what happened, but when I went to see her later, she was crying…"

"So you wanted to hurt him?"

"Yes."

"Did this happen a lot?"

"I don't know. I only saw her the one time."

"Could that have been what your mother wanted to tell you in your dream, when you dropped your grandson?"

"Tell me what?"

"That she was in danger?"

"I don't know. I think she wanted to help me protect my grandson… Maybe she wanted to warn me about what happened to her…maybe she was worrying about my grandson."

"Is it possible that there's something about her death that you don't know?"

"Maybe…that's what my friend is hoping to find out."

"What if—unconsciously—you've always worried that something happened to your mother. But it was unconscious, you repressed it, you never let yourself be aware of it. When your grandson was born, these worries surfaced, they had a way to get out. Only the worry was displaced—reassigned to your grandson. There was no real threat to your grandson, but it brought up feelings from your own childhood, that your mother was in danger, that someone actually wanted to hurt her."

"Is that possible?"

"I can't answer that positively, but is it possible? Yes…either way, it's a heavy load to carry."

"Are you saying that my whole life I hid, I buried, my idea that maybe my mother and father didn't die in an accident?"

"You wanted to hurt your father. You were afraid that your parents were killed as a punishment for your angry feelings. Most of this is a child's irrational worry. But—you had reason to worry about your mother's safety. In your dreams as an adult, your mother is trying to tell you something. Something alarming enough that you would drop your baby grandson. Now, we're only guessing. What we need to do is to find out precisely what your mother is trying to tell you."

"I have no idea."

"That's what we have to work on. You're the only person in the world who can answer that question."

"I don't know how to do that, and it scares me."

"It should, and still, I believe that one day, you'll be able to tell us what she's saying."

"This is not at all what I expected in therapy. It's totally outside of my experience."

"No, though you don't know it yet, *it is your experience*, yours alone, and you've lived it, hidden away in your mind, your whole life."

◆◆◆

Cash, Callie, Sara, Alvaro, and Andre were sitting at Callie's table upstairs in the corner beside the bar. Young Cash was sleeping peacefully in a crib they'd set up nearby. He seemed to be able to tune out the talking, even the occasional laughing. Andre was explaining what he'd learned today.

"It took forever to find the files, and when we finally did, they seemed to tell the same story that you told me years ago. The police and the coroner on the case concurred that your dad was driving drunk. His drunkenness caused the accident."

"Anything new in the file?"

"About six months ago, someone looked at it. The name he used was John Franklin, but that meant nothing to me."

"Can you find out who he is?"

"I'm already on it, but it's a common name, and so far, it's going nowhere."

"An alias?"

"That's my guess. I'll make another pass, but don't hold your breath."

"Okay, let me know if you find anything… Did you reread the descriptions of my mom and dad, particularly how they identified them?"

"Same as you said. Your mom's boss recognized her right away. Two reliable witnesses identified your dad easily, confirming his particular dental work, a monogrammed flask, and a driver's license. He also had high alcohol in his blood. Everything checked out. I'm going back tomorrow, meeting with a medical examiner I know. I'm wondering if he can answer a question I had about the write up of your mother."

"What was your question?"

"The coroner who did the autopsy of your mom indicated that there was an injury that could have happened before the accident, a bad bruise on her face and another on her back. He couldn't come to a conclusion about the one on her face because she also had bruises on her face from the accident. The one on her back, however, he couldn't explain. He concluded that it was likely from an accident and never pursued it any further. He was a coroner, though, not a medical examiner. I want to explore that with a medical examiner that I know from Seattle."

"Yes, thank you. That could be important."

"He's agreed to meet me there. He's thorough and tenacious."

"Please keep me posted."

"Of course." Andre turned to Sara. "How's my favorite young lady?"

"Tired. Baby Cash doesn't always sleep so well." Sara pointed at her son, sleeping soundly.

"He's much better looking than his grandfather. You already have that going for him."

"Don't provoke my dad," Sara suggested. She put a hand on her dad's shoulder. "He's quick to anger these days."

"Getting angry at Andre is like spitting into the wind." Cash noted ruefully.

Alvaro looked up, serious. "Cash, you seem perfectly fine, normal. You're also a very smart guy. Can you tell us anything about what turns you into an irrational, out-of-control, angry bully? I'm sure you're thinking about it, talking with your therapist. Do you mind talking about that?"

"No, I'm okay talking about it with all of you, even Andre." Cash looked at him, sternly. "But I really don't understand it… What I think is that ever since Young Cash was born, I've been worrying about his safety. It's irrational; he's well taken care of, and no one has put him in danger. My therapist suggested that my grandson being born could be just the spark for me worrying about my own childhood, particularly my mother. I've been having dreams about her. In my dreams, she's about to say something to me when I drop my grandson, unknowingly. When I pick him up, he's hurt but still alive. Before I can even calm him down, my mother is gone."

"What about this makes you angry?" Callie asked.

"I don't know. When I get angry, it's for no good reason, and I can't control it."

"Could you be angry because you feel helpless, unable to protect your grandson?" Callie asked. "I can only imagine how hard that would be for you."

"Maybe. But what my therapist got me thinking about is what if I'm angry about my mother being in danger. What if I'm helpless to protect her? After all, when I was seven years old, she died in an accident, and I wasn't able to do anything to stop it."

"How could you?" Sara asked. "You were just seven years old."

"Ach…sorry…but this is starting to bother me…I'm getting a headache, and that's the first thing I feel before I get really angry." Cash put his hands to his temples. "Damnit. I have to leave. Now." He got up and left the room hurriedly, going down into the kitchen.

Sara signaled to Callie. "Let me go after him. I think I know something about how he's feeling."

Callie nodded. "Please call me if I can help."

Sara hurried down after her dad.

◆◆◆

When Sara came into the kitchen, her dad was sitting at the maple prep table, he had his head in his hands.

Sara came behind him, put a hand on each shoulder, and then began massaging his neck with both hands. "Do you want me to bring you some aspirin?" she asked.

Cash nodded. She could see that he was tearing up.

Sara took a bottle of Tylenol from the pantry, got a glass of water, and then came back to her dad. "Try this," she whispered.

Cash took two Tylenols, drank them down with a drink of water.

Sara said, "Please let me talk dad, you don't have to say anything. Please just listen."

Cash went back to pressing his temples.

Sara came back behind him and began massaging his neck again with both hands. She clearly knew what she was doing. Cash felt it and took a slow breath.

"I have some idea about how you're feeling," she said. "In the orphanage, before I escaped, I would get depressed. I didn't really understand it then, but when I was older, after I escaped, it started happening again, even worse. It happened off and on, unpredictably, over several years. What I remember was feeling totally hopeless, unable to feel better. I'd get painful headaches, like yours. Sometimes, I would get very angry, angry at myself. I would even think about killing myself. But I had my father's genes. I made myself spend time alone in the tiny basement room they loaned me in their old café in the Algerian ghetto in Marseilles. I massaged my own neck, listened to music. Anything that would make the sadness and the horrible headaches go away. I imagine you feel something like that."

Cash took one of her hands on his neck, held it, squeezed it tightly.

"Please let me help you, Dad. There's nothing to feel ashamed about. It's horrible to feel hopeless, completely helpless. Please talk to me about how hard it feels, about how you lose who you are. I can't fix it, but I can make it more bearable."

Cash took her other hand, turned, and stood to hold her in his arms. He was tearing up now, holding her head on his shoulder. "Thank you, my lovely daughter. For your awareness, for your understanding."

"There's nothing like it. I know."

"It's been worse than I let on. Although I don't say this, getting angry is almost a relief."

"I get that… Do you think your therapist can help?"

"I hope so, but I don't know."

"I found my mother when I was fourteen, at my worst. It changed everything. She listened to me, helped me come back. Please let me be there for you. I can't bring you back, but I can help you bear it while you work it out with your therapist."

"That would be a relief for me. At the very least, it will help me with the headaches. Maybe help me be somehow more balanced and at least a little more in control. It's taking me too much time and energy, becoming too difficult, hiding the pain, the hopelessness. Letting it out with you might help."

"I'll help you with that, Dad. I can do that."

CHAPTER TWO

Cash was sitting in the worn leather chair facing Abe. He was trying to explain what had happened with Sara and how much it had meant to him.

"She's a sensitive, thoughtful young woman. She's always surprising me. I was talking about therapy, and Alvaro, Sara's husband, asked if I had any idea why I got so angry. I responded, saying, 'What my therapist got me thinking about is what if I'm angry about my mother being in danger. What if I was helpless to protect her? After all, when I was seven years old, she died in an accident, and I wasn't able to do anything to stop it.'

"'How could you?' my daughter asked. 'You were just seven years old?'

"And I started to unwind. Bad headache, edgy, all the symptoms I recognize. So I excused myself and went downstairs to the kitchen. Not two minutes later, my daughter was there, massaging my neck, telling me how she recognized this. She grew up in an orphanage, and she used to get very depressed. She described feelings that were a version of mine. The thing was that talking about it with her was actually helpful. She told me that she couldn't solve it—that was up to me and my therapist. But she said that she could help me get through it. It was a sincere offer, and I think she could actually help. We talked for almost an hour last night. I mostly talked, and she listened and asked questions. They were smart questions. It helped me unwind, be less fearful. It made me feel less alone. She does understand what it feels like to be overwhelmed by your own frustrating, inexplicably angry feelings, your sense of helplessness in the face of it. She gets how it makes you distant and ashamed, especially with the people you most care about. Talking with my daughter like this is new for me."

"That's a lovely turn of events. Being able to share what you're feeling with your daughter, a person who's known similar issues, is a gift."

"It won't solve the problem, though."

"That's true but having real support while you're working it out—frustrated, discouraged, worrying that you're stuck—that's invaluable. And it's an important statement about you, about your relationship with your daughter, that she's willing to do this."

"It made me want to figure this out. Made me more hopeful, so let's you and I do our best. Truthfully, I'm more optimistic."

"Fair enough. If you're okay with it, I'd like to go back to what your mother might have been hoping to say in your dream?"

"That's fine."

"Good. Here's what I'm wondering. Suppose your mother was trying to tell you that she was in danger?"

"Why would she be saying that to a seven-year-old boy?"

"She's not. You are. And you're saying it as a forty-eight-year-old man in a dream. Why do you think you're doing that?"

"Maybe I'm trying to undo my seven-year-old mistake."

"Interesting, can you be more specific?"

"I didn't protect her then, maybe I can at least protect my grandson now."

"But your grandson doesn't need protection. What did your mother need?"

"If I'd done something, maybe she'd still be alive."

"Done what? She died in an accident."

"What if it wasn't an accident?"

"What was it?"

"I don't know..."

"Take your best guess..."

"I can't imagine what it was, if it wasn't an accident...and can we take a break? I'm getting a headache."

"Please let me try one more time. Suppose it wasn't an accident, but no one knew that. If it wasn't an accident, what was she trying to say?"

Cash massaged his neck. "What if she wanted to say that I died in an accident, and no one ever knew that it wasn't an accident."

"Yes. Yes. At seven years old, you worried that your mother may have been killed, even if it was made to look like an accident."

"Why would I think that?"

"I think as a child, you saw that your mother needed protection. Someone, likely your father, was hurting her. Then, whether it was an accident or not, someone killed her. After she died, you wondered if you could have done something to save her. It was unbearable for you to think that, so you repressed it…and then your grandson was born—"

"And I start dreaming about my mother. We're now supposing that in my dream, she's trying to tell me what happened to her. She does that by warning me that my grandson could die and his murderer could make it look like an accident. Isn't that quite a long reach, full of guesses and speculations?"

"Yes, it is, but it's not necessarily real. It's what's in your unconscious. It doesn't have to be what happened. For now, what matters is that you, today, for years, have repressed a childhood worry that someone killed your mother."

"When I was seven years old?"

"Yes, when your mother died."

"I wouldn't have believed that a week ago…" Cash frowned, pensive.

"Go slowly now. Very carefully. Just because you worried about it at seven doesn't mean that it really happened."

"But I do think that now. I need to learn as much as possible about what actually happened."

"That won't be easy. It was over forty years ago."

"This kind of work is something my friends and I are good at. I'm going to call Andre this afternoon and talk details with him tonight."

"Please keep me posted."

"You can count on it."

◆◆◆

Kit came out of the back of Grand Central onto Vanderbilt. He turned left, walking south toward Forty-Second, when his phone rang. He tensed, it was Mr. Li.

"Where are you?" were the first words he heard.

"Behind Grand Central, on Vanderbilt."

"Walk up the street to Forty-Fourth. On the northwest corner, you'll see a building, The Yale Club. Wait in front. I'll pick you up there in five minutes."

"The Yale Club?" Kit asked, confused, but by then, Mr. Li was already gone. He looked toward Forty-Fourth, across at the old building with the blue awning with the logo—a letter Y superimposed on top of a C—printed on three sides, one in front and one on each side. Well above the awning, slightly north, hung a blue flag with the big white letter Y on it. Kit wondered how Mr. Li knew a place like that. He guessed that Chen had killed someone who was staying there, someone who owed him money. Though Kit had never paid attention to this club, he wasn't surprised that the dangerous son of a bitch knew someone staying at a place like that. Kit crossed the street and leaned back against the old gray stone building, just south of the blue awning.

The car, a black Mercedes, arrived two minutes later. When the door opened, Kit sat in the back seat beside Mr. Chen Li. Mr. Chen Li was wider—he weighed 235 pounds—and even taller than Kit at 6'2". He was a strong-looking, intimidating man. Chen had pressed a button that caused a tinted gray glass to partially separate them from the driver and another man, likely one of Chen's lieutenants, who sat in the front seat. This man was well-dressed and carried a gun in his right hand. The gun was pointed at Kit through the open portion of the tinted glass.

"I didn't know that you were here," Kit finally said. He tried not to stare at the massive, unusually large Chinese man; it was hard.

"I have some business here. I timed my trip to be soon after your release. I'm sure you know why I'm here."

"We should be able to pay you within one month."

"I've waited eleven years. I want payment within ten days, not a day more."

Kit looked at the gun, still pointed at his chest. "We will pay you before the deadline."

"There's one other matter."

"What other matter?"

"Interest."

Kit tensed. "What interest?"

"I will be charging four percent on $7,000,000 for almost eleven years."

"Is this a joke?" Kit did the math. "That's $3,080,000... Are you crazy?" Kit regretted saying that as soon as the words came out of his mouth.

Chen Li had a knife, a double-edged blade stiletto pressed against the back of Kit's left ear. "If you didn't owe me $10,080,000, you would be dead now. If you ever ask me an insulting question like that again, I will increase the interest to six percent, then, once you've paid, I will kill you. Do you understand?"

"I do. I apologize for my thoughtless, foolish question. It won't ever happen again."

Chen nodded. "Yes, I will make sure that it won't." With a deft, swift motion, Chen cut off Kit's left ear with the stiletto in his right hand. Chen had a handkerchief in his left hand, and he caught the severed ear in the handkerchief.

Chen watched, his blade now pressed against Kit's neck, as Kit was unable to stifle a fierce scream. Kit used his own handkerchief to slow the bleeding from his missing left ear, as he screamed again.

Chen nodded, pleased at Kit's pain. He added, "I will expect my payment within ten days—it's actually several months less than eleven years. I'll generously call it $10,000,000. I will preserve your lost ear. If you pay my money timely, I will return it. With any luck and a skillful surgeon, you can have it reattached. Do you understand?"

Kit took a moment, catching his breath, then he nodded, his hand still holding the bloody handkerchief to his missing ear. "Yes, I understand," he said softly, carefully.

Chen Li said something in Chinese to the driver, who pulled the car over. Chen said, "Our business is completed. You may leave."

After the man in the front seat, Chen's lieutenant, opened the door, he offered a hand to Kit and helped him out of the back seat. The man was well dressed. He wore an expensive pin-stripe suit and a handsome silk tie. His gun was visible in a fine-looking brown leather holster under his left shoulder. He walked Kit to a bus stop nearby, where he sat him on the bench. He leaned down to whisper into what used to be Kit's left ear. "You're lucky. You only lost an ear. Could have been your—what is your quaint colloquialism—*Johnson*, yes, yes, your precious *Johnson*." The man nodded, then he returned to the car.

Kit watched the Mercedes leave, watching Mr. Chen Li, who was already doing other business on his cell phone. Kit screamed again, loudly, as he pressed his red handkerchief to the spot on his left side where his ear used to be. It was still bleeding. Chen was, demonstrably, the most dangerous man he'd ever met. Kit was not easily frightened, but just remembering Chen scared him. Still, Kit considered killing Mr. Chen Li tonight. Even if, unlikely, he was able to find him, he knew he was unlikely to succeed. If, against all odds, he did kill him, one of Chen's Hong Kong Triads cohorts, like the menacing armed man in the front seat, would come after him tomorrow. No, he'd raise the ransom, pay his money plus interest, then later, when Chen had forgotten about him, Kit would fool him, a thing he knew how to do. Yes, he'd lure him into a skillfully designed trap, then he'd kill him, slowly. Before he died, he'd make him taste the shame.

◆◆◆

Andre was waiting at Shuckers Oyster Bar, a seafood restaurant in the Fairmount Hotel, when Cash arrived. It had beautifully carved oak paneling and a unique tin ceiling. Andre had taken a remote table, set apart by the window, and he was happily working on eighteen oysters, Kumamotos and Hamamotos served on ice on a plate with two small spoons in a bowl of their mignonette sauce, made with red wine vinegar and minced shallots, in the center. Their friend and often collaborator, Lieutenant Detective Ed Samter, was eating oysters with him.

Cash smiled at his friends, "Ciao," he said.

"You look better," Ed noted. "Abe Stein must be earning his money."

"He better work fast. No shrink could possibly last more than two weeks with Cash," Andre announced. "I know this like a salmon knows where to spawn."

Cash popped the back of Andre's head playfully, then sat down and helped himself to a Kumamoto. After pouring on a small spoonful of the mignonette, he sucked the oyster out of the shell. "Excellent," he declared.

Andre nodded, finishing a Hamamoto and taking another.

"What did you find?" Cash asked.

"My medical examiner friend said the coroner was not very careful. Specifically, there was no follow-up on the bruises on your mom's back, nor an autopsy of either your mom or your dad. That's why I asked Ed to join us." Andre nodded at the detective, who took over.

"I know the higher-ups in the police department in Tacoma," Ed explained. "After Andre filled me in, I talked with a judge, then pulled in some favors. They've given us the go-ahead to dig up what's left of both bodies. They can do it the day after tomorrow. I don't think we'll learn much from your mother's remains, though if she was hurt before the accident, if there were any broken bones, they may show up. I have no idea what your father's body has to tell us, but we'll take a look."

"Well done, gentleman. That's what I was hoping for. What I'm exploring with Abe Stein is the notion that this wasn't an accident. This isn't based on any proof, it's mostly psycho hocus pocus, but I like him, I think he's smart, and I think he may be on to something. Let's find out."

Samter nodded. "He's not only smart, he's counterintuitive, and he sees things that a lot of us miss. I must say, though, I'd bet that our spawning salmon is right about his timeline, that is to say that Abe's patience for helping you could be running out."

Cash ignored him. "What time day after tomorrow?"

"They'll deliver what's left of the bodies to an examining room, day after tomorrow in the afternoon. I wrote down the place." Samter showed them the address. "That's where your medical examiner friend can take a look."

Andre turned to Cash. "The medical examiner asked if there were any old medical records of your father?"

"I have both my father's and my mother's medical records. My grandparents gave them to me before they died. They saved them in case I ever had a medical problem. I have them put away in a safe upstairs. I'll also get a blood test to compare DNA."

"Good." Andre went on, "There's a Tacoma cop who's still alive who was at the scene. He's at a long-term care home. I've arranged to see him tomorrow morning."

"All good. Thank you both. This is giving me a headache, so I'm going home to unwind. Call me anytime if you need anything."

Andre couldn't resist, "You were a lot easier to work with when you weren't such a pussy."

"I may have turned into a pussy, but you better hope I don't get angry at you. I can still kick your ass."

Samter was watching the two of them, realizing that this kind of banter was just part of their fondness for one another. "You guys ought to tone it down. If I didn't know better, I'd think you hated each other."

They both turned to Detective Samter and said at the same time, "We do."

◆◆◆

Cash was sleeping next to Callie. They had an oversized king bed that they shared in the apartment. Still, the bed wasn't quite big enough when Cash didn't sleep well. Tonight, he was having a nightmare. In his dream, his dad was looking for him, angry. He hid in the shed, outside, but his dad found him, put him over the bench in the shed, and beat him with his belt. He beat him harshly, causing welts to form on his legs, his bottom, and his back. While he beat Cash, he ranted, calling him a useless, incompetent, wretched child. Cash woke up, short of breath, frightened, until he realized he'd been dreaming. He took a minute to think about his dream. As far as he knew, his dad had never whipped him with his belt. He'd remember that if it had happened. Why, he wondered, was he afraid of that. His dad was mean; he'd often cursed at him, and one time, he'd hit him, but nothing like the beating in this nightmare.

Callie leaned over, put her hand on his shoulder. "Bad dream?"

"Yeah."

"That's unusual for you. You want to talk about it?"

"No, I'm okay. Maybe in the morning."

Callie kissed his cheek fondly, then turned over.

Cash took her hand. When he was breathing normally, he went back to sleep, unsettled.

◆◆◆

Cash was waiting for Abe in the waiting room at 9:00 a.m.. When he opened the door, Cash went straight to his chair, sat down, and began describing his dream. When he was finished, Abe asked, "Have you ever had this dream before?"

"Not that I know of. I rarely remember my dreams, though, if I even have them."

"Have you ever had any similar dream or another version of this dream?"

"Not that I know of."

"Any idea why you had this dream, presumably for the first time, last night?"

"I was wondering about that. The only thing I could think of was how we're digging up his remains today to examine them."

"Do you imagine he might be mad about that?"

"Absolutely, he used to get mad for any excuse he could find. He had unpredictable bursts of anger. He'd scream at me for imagined mistakes, like stealing money from his wallet when that had never happened… never…"

“He sounds like a frightening, possibly dangerous father.”

“With hindsight, he was. When I was seven, after I found my mother crying in her room, I told a teacher at school that I was worried about my mother, about her bruises.”

“What happened?”

“I was at school, but the next day, a policeman came to my house to check out my mom. I wasn’t there, but they convinced the policeman that she’d had an accident. My mom must have gone along with it.”

“Did you hear about it later?”

“There’s more. I also told the teacher that I overheard them fighting about hiding cases in the basement. When I got home from school that day, the two of them sat me down and explained that it had been an accident, that the cases had been returned to the port. Even then, I thought my mother was lying. My father was trying to be nice, at least polite, but whenever I looked in his eyes, I thought he might hurt me.”

“Did he ever hurt you again?”

“No. He calmed down. Still, I avoided him, and my mother protected me from him.”

“I can imagine how digging up his remains might bring back being afraid of him.”

“Yeah. But he’s dead, so he won’t know.”

“Is it possible that you’re worried that he isn’t dead?”

“Why would I be worried about that?”

“It may not be conscious. It may be a child’s worry, a worry that if he killed your mother and got away with it, then he might be able to fake his own death and get away with that too.”

“If my dad isn’t dead, what’s he been doing for the past forty-one years?”

“Good question.”

“It seems very unlikely, and you seem more and more prone to—excuse my phrase—psychobabble. Killed my mother and faked his own death, and get away with that for forty-one years? You’ve spent too much time imagining what’s going on in people’s minds that they don’t know about.”

"That may be true, but since you're digging up his body today, you might discover more about that."

"Or put it to rest."

"Either way, it's progress."

"This is not making me feel any better. I'm feeling helpless, depressed, my headache is back, I'm getting angry with you, and I don't have any sense that this facile theorizing is helping me."

Abe nodded, raised his palms. "Cash Logan, I'm asking you to do me a favor—please pay careful attention to what I have to say."

Cash jumped in, vaguely hostile. "I always pay attention, and if I'm not, I'm still paying for your time."

"I know you're angry, and you don't mean to be hurtful, but please, just listen to me…" He waited until he had Cash's full attention. "I may be completely wrong about this whole direction of inquiries, but I'm very experienced at uncovering hard-to-reach things. Your hostility, your resistance suggests that we may be touching a nerve. I want you to trust me, to endure what I'm sure is genuine unpleasantness. I wouldn't be pressing this if it wasn't important. I won't ever try to convince you to believe something you don't think is true, but I'm wondering if you saw something that reminded you of your father. It could be a coat, an old bicycle, a hat, or a briefcase, but that might have started some of this—the worry about what happened to your mother—think about your dream last night, your father whipping you, yelling at you."

Cash touched Abe's forearm across the table, took a slow breath. "Damn you! Of course…you're so smart that I should be able to do better with you, at least, get better at trusting you… I'm sorry. Please forgive me."

"Don't worry about that. What made you calm down? It's like your anger slowed down, dissipated, as quickly as it took over."

"You were right about something I didn't even think about until this moment. Three days ago, when I was walking to see Detective Samter, the man who told me about your history with Nick Season, I saw an older man crossing the street at First and Pine. He was wearing a worn leather jacket and a classic vintage green and red Seattle Supersonics hat. It had a red brim, and on the green top of the hat stood the old orange, red, and green Sonics emblem. In the middle of the emblem the Seattle Space Needle rose in white. My father always wore a Seattle Sonic hat like that and an old leather jacket. This was back in the early eighties, when I was six or seven. I don't think this was my father, but he looked a little like an older version of how I remembered him."

"What did you think when you saw him?"

"I got angry with Howard Schultz, the Starbucks owner who bought the Sonics and then sold them in 2008 to a group that moved them to Oklahoma City."

"You didn't think about your dad?"

"No. I remembered an old Seattle hat like that, one that I owned later. But no, I didn't think about my dad until just now..." Cash hesitated. "This is going pretty fast. I'm sorry, it's hard for me to keep up."

"You don't ever need to apologize. You're wrestling with difficult, complicated things, and we don't really know yet what's real. You're still working very hard, struggling with your own anger, as well as new material that's forty-one years old. Give yourself some credit; you're doing just fine."

"That's nice of you to say, but I'm feeling like I'm in a fog. None of this has any reality to me except in my shifting, almost impossible to remember, childish memory."

"That's absolutely normal. All that we can do right now is to explore what a seven-year-old might have imagined. Hopefully, when they examine the remains of the bodies, we'll be able to learn more about our questions. Are we certain that it was an accident? Was your mother injured before the accident? Was the man in the car actually your father? If any of the answers to these questions are what we fear, you have a lot of work to do now, in the present. If these worries aren't real, alternatively, if we establish them as nothing more than childhood fantasies, you can move on. At the very least, if none of it is real, we can focus on other things that might be upsetting you."

"My head is spinning. I'm usually way ahead of other people. With you, it's all I can do to stay in the conversation."

"Let's take a break. Tomorrow, you'll take a look at the bodies… Please call me after you see the bodies. If you'd like to come in and talk more, I'll find some way to work that out… It will take at least another day to run the tests they'll want completed. Let's definitely regroup then, the day after tomorrow afternoon."

"That sounds good."

"Thanks for listening. I know it wasn't easy."

"No, it wasn't, but truthfully, I'm lucky to have you working with me. Please remind me that I said that the next time I get angry."

"Thank you."

♦♦♦

Kit was waiting at the bar at the Oyster Bar Saloon, downstairs in Grand Central Station. Gus always came in on the train, so Grand Central was their preferred meeting spot. To find the Saloon, first, you had to know how to find the restaurant. You look for the six metal-framed glass doors under the marble arch at the bottom of the ramp on the Vanderbilt side, opposite the train tracks. In the arch itself, bold brown letters spell out OYSTER BAR RESTAURANT. All six doors open into the sizeable restaurant.

The Saloon, a 1920s-era bar and dining hall, can be reached through the far-right back corner of the OYSTER BAR RESTAURANT. The hundred-year-old Oyster Bar Restaurant is a vast, lively room that is often crowded and always, always smells like fish. Its best feature—the beautiful, vaulted ceilings—is covered with Guastavino terracotta tiles set in a herringbone pattern. Once inside, you have to turn north and hike to the right rear corner of the large, fish-scented space to find the simple, wooden swinging saloon door.

It was always a treat when you stepped inside the tavern—red and white checkered tablecloths, warm, dark woods, chairs trimmed with rustic brass nail heads. To the right, a handsome, winding mahogany bar made an L along the north and east sides of the restaurant. Models and photos of multi-mast sailing ships hung from the walls. Kit had found two seats at the bar in the far-right corner—under the mounted tarpon at the very top of the L—and ordered two Bombay Blue Sapphire Gin martinis, extra dry, with olives. Gus arrived as the martinis were served, each one with an extra inch of a refill in a glass tumbler. "The angel's share," Kit explained. He wore a white patch over his left ear.

Gus looked at his patch, "Chen cut off your ear?"

"You're too smart, Gus… Yes, damnit. The feral bastard said he'd give it back if we gave him his money plus four percent interest for eleven years. He rounded it off to $10,000,000. He expects it in ten days."

"Shit…no choice…right?"

"We will surely be killed if we don't."

"Can we kill him first?"

"Until we pay his money, it would be easier to kill the president. I'm thinking that after, I may be able to trick him into a trap. I'm not sure it's worth the risk, especially since we'll never get the money back. That said, he has to die slowly, taste his own shame, before I'm done with him. Period."

"Matter of pride."

"I know that counts for you. I don't give a shit about pride. This is retribution. The arrogant sadist can't take my ear. I'm going to cut off his peanut-sized dick before I kill him."

"That's my guy, and boss, I got to say, I'm sensing a little bit of pride in there too."

"You can call it whatever the fuck you want."

"Okay, let's leave it there—I'll call it pride, you can call it retribution or dick removal or any damn thing you want. Can we move on?"

"I'm going to make him swallow his dick after I cut it off. Maybe I'll find a sick old whore, make him eat spoiled, puss-dripping pussy."

"Whoa, the incomparable silver-tongued Devil has spoken. You can relax, boss, you're the king. I know you'll make him taste unforgettable shame. I've seen you do that to people who bother you. Remember Jimmy Stone, inside? He tasted the shame like that before he died."

"Yes, he did…he certainly did…"

"Glory to God!"

"I'm feeling better," Kit said.

"Okay, good… Should we increase the ransom?"

"$18,000,000. Is that a problem?"

"I don't think so, and we'll still walk away with $4,000,000 each."

"Right. It does mean we'll have to speed everything up, go into action tomorrow."

"That's no problem. I can be in Seattle tonight."

"As we planned, I'm assuming you won't need me in phase one?"

"No, as you know, I've got two excellent men in place. As I told you, the safe house is already set up."

"We'll need to make the ransom demand the day after tomorrow evening, latest. I'll handle that."

"Will you come to Seattle?"

"Only if I have to. If I set it up right, I can receive the money in Geneva, then pay Chen's share from there."

"As we planned."

"Exactly. We've been over and over this, examining every outcome, every possible misstep. Nothing has been left to chance." Kit raised his martini.

Gus toasted, "Ten days to glory…"

Kit touched his glass, took another sip of his martini. "I'm beginning to anticipate the sweet taste of inflicting shame…feel the savory satisfaction of exacting unthinkable, shocking retribution… First, let's taste great wealth!"

"To riches…to glory!"

♦♦♦

The Macher arrived on his jet at SeaTac at 5:00, and he was scheduled to meet them at his favorite Seattle restaurant, The Bronze Pig. It was a surprise birthday party for Cash. Sara had planned the evening to celebrate her dad's forty-ninth birthday. It was a Monday night, so the restaurant was closed. For the occasion, Césaire had agreed to cook, Jill had insisted on tending bar, and Will had come in to help in any way he could. Callie was not working tonight. She was planning on celebrating with her beloved, albeit unhappy, partner. Although she worried he'd have an angry episode, she was hoping that the surprise birthday party, with his best friends there, would be a break from his depression.

Cash was due to come down from their apartment at 7:00. He was expecting to meet Callie at the kitchen, and then go out with her to a special place she'd organized for the occasion. Sara had been there since 3:00, decorating the dining area for the party with Lew's help. They'd put up a collection of photos taken of Cash with all of his adopted family, his friends, and friends from around the world. There was even a large blown-up picture of Cash holding his baby grandson that Sara had taken, unbeknownst to him, soon after Baby Cash was born. The photos were carefully placed on the wall, the oversized photo prominently set in the center, beside the cherry wood mullioned picture window—the restored front window that Daniel, Callie's ex, had been blown threw, after being hit by a truck, purposely, years ago. She and Lew had hung festive decorations—balloons, crepe paper streamers, ribbons, twinkle stars, and a colorful banner saying, "Happy Birthday Cash!" They'd even hung multicolored lights up the stairs to the loft and over the loft itself. Andre and Jill were already setting up a bar downstairs. Andre, of course, had all the fixing for his exotic cocktails from Vientiane, Tangier, Port-au-Prince, and so on, presented in several bags hung from netsuke, Japanese erotic carvings, used to suspend bags from their sashes attached to their Kimonos. Cash had smuggled the netsukes into the restaurant long ago. Alvaro held sleeping Baby Cash in his arms, sitting in a chair at the large table that had been set in the dining room for the festive dinner. He offered suggestions, often unwanted, but politely received.

Between the large table and the booths, tables had been removed to provide a comfortable area for dancing. In that corner, a piano and a microphone had been set up for singing.

At 6:30, guests started arriving. Sara had a long reach, helped by how much people liked Cash, so she'd invited out-of-town people from NYC, LA, Haiti, and even Cuba. Most of the people invited were coming. Lew's lovely girlfriend, Lisa, was first, then Sergeant Lincoln and his wife Cherry, who came with Detective Ed Samter and his girlfriend, soon-to-be wife, Kate. Next came Nestor, from Cuba, with his family—his wife, Lilliana, his daughter, Alicia, and her husband, Camilo. Soon after came Eva, Sara's doctor in Cuba, who'd stayed in touch and became a friend, seeing Sara both in Cuba and in Miami. She especially liked Alvaro's nightclub. The Macher's arrival brought cheers and warm hugs all around. Junior and Samuel, Haitian crew members from the so-called Haitian Coast Guard vessel that hijacked Sara's kidnapper's yacht, were last. They'd successfully taken the kidnappers on the yacht to face prison in Cuba. They'd gone on to work for Andre, a subject that was never described in detail, and, as often happened, they'd stayed friends with Cash.

Callie got all of their attention with a clicked glass, welcomed them, and asked them to hide in the soon-to-be dark dining room until she and Cash came in from the kitchen. She'd lead him in, turn on the light, and then it was time to sing, for the first time, "Happy Birthday."

At 7:05, Cash and Callie came out from the kitchen in the darkness to an empty dining room. When she turned on the lights, the crowd appeared from the dark alcoves, almost magically. In the lights, the decorations were lovely, and the loud singing of "Happy Birthday" to Cash was joyous and heartfelt.

Cash was completely surprised, and as he looked around the room, recognizing the friendly faces, his eyes filled with tears. His daughter flew into his arms, and he hugged her. Somehow, he knew that Sara had planned this, and he whispered, "I love you. Thank you," in her ear. When she led him by the arm to see the photo with his grandson, he burst into tears of joy. He turned to see so many friends cheering for him, and he said, "Thank you, all of you. Thank you so much. You have no idea how much this means to me." Cash walked through the crowd, touching arms, hugging people, simply enjoying being surrounded by friends. Before he could embrace them all, Alvaro had his grandson in his arms, and Cash was surrounded by everyone to take a group picture with the proud birthday grandfather. Will took the picture; Sara, Callie, and Lew were somehow all around him. Callie thought that she hadn't seen him feeling so good in a long time.

Callie and Will led them to the table, where people sat wherever they wanted. It took a while because so many people hadn't seen each other since they were at a party here to celebrate Sara's return from Cuba after getting her identity back. That was almost two years ago. Nestor was particularly excited to see his friends again, as were Eva and Lincoln. Sara, along with Callie, were splendid hostesses, going from place to place, making sure people were settled in comfortably.

Césaire announced a formidable dinner featuring foie gras with pear sauce, Potage Lyonnaise, truffle risotto, Copper River salmon, and cassoulet with game sausages, in honor of Doc. He stopped for Cash to say a word and others to take a moment of silence to honor Cash's lost friend. Those who knew him, knew that he was with them tonight.

When Césaire finished, the Macher stepped up, lifting a glass to simply say, "It's an honor to be celebrating such an important occasion with such a wonderful man. He's a fantastic husband, a remarkable father, and a soon-to-be legendary grandfather. Equally important, I think we'll all agree, is that he's a remarkable, remarkable, friend. Bravo, Cash Logan!" Thunderous applause, clapping, and shouting filled the room. Everyone stood up for a moment to applaud, to celebrate their dear friend.

As it died down, Sara came to the microphone, the Macher sat at the piano, and Cash joined her for a rousing version of Willie Nelson's rendition of "Crazy." It was already a spectacular party, and it was just getting started.

CHAPTER THREE

The party had gone on into the late night and then early morning. There were many remembrances of Cash, Callie, Andre, and, of course, Sara. People particularly loved Cash's rendition of how Sara saved his life, leaping off a parked car through the air to kill a dangerous assassin before he could kill Cash. Eva joined in describing their condition when she saw both of them later that night, and Nestor was especially touching as he described both of them staying in his house the following days. Itzac, the Macher, told stories about getting to know Sara, and, of course, recounting how Cash's extraordinary strategic abilities fashioned the plan that was able to get back Sara's stolen identity. Around 4:00 in the morning, people began to leave, but not before Sara and Alvaro displayed some very classy Salsa dancing.

Cash slept late—9:00 was late for him—and woke up feeling great. Callie was still asleep, so he quietly got dressed in their bathroom, then went down to the kitchen, had his coffee, and went out for a walk. He liked to walk alone in the mornings; it helped him get organized for the day. He was going down the alley behind the kitchen when he was approached by two well-dressed, middle-aged men looking for directions. One, the taller man, was African American. His friend was Caucasian, shorter, and red-haired. They looked like out-of-towners, maybe New York City, and Cash stopped to look at their map. He was looking at the "X" on the map when he felt two barbs, dart-like electrodes from a taser, strike his chest. The electrodes created a circuit in the body, essentially hijacking the central nervous system, causing neuromuscular incapacitation. He tried to defend himself, but it was too late. He fell to the alley, writhing in uncontrollable muscle spasms. When he curled into the fetal position, the men cuffed his hands behind his back, and then roughly carried him into the trunk of their car. In the car trunk, the red-haired man poured some chloroform on a rag and covered it on Cash's mouth and nose. He took it off briefly, to give him another drug, diazepam, then replaced the chloroform until he was unconscious. When he was out, they closed the trunk.

When Cash woke up, he was in a basement, he supposed, chained to a wall. He was blindfolded, so he couldn't see anything, but he remembered waking up briefly, confused, being hauled down the stairs. He guessed that there was one light bulb lit on the ceiling, though he couldn't see it. He'd heard a chain pulled when he came down the stairs. Excepting the metal folding chair he sat on, he had no idea if there was any other furniture in the room. He was uncomfortable. Both of his arms were above his head, his wrists securely handcuffed to the wall. He felt groggy, unsettled; aftereffects, he imagined, from the taser darts and the shot in the back of his neck. No one had told him anything, and he was alone. He tried to imagine why he'd been taken. He had no idea.

◆◆◆

Kit was in the one-bedroom apartment he'd rented under an assumed name in an inconspicuous old building in the Lower Eastside. He was talking to Gus on the phone. "So far, so good," he said in response to Gus's report.

"What should I tell him?"

"Tell him nothing. Nothing at all. Keep him blindfolded. If he never sees you or any of the other men, that's perfect. I'll send the ransom note as soon as you take a photo and send it to me. I don't think the next phase of this will take long."

"You make it seem easy."

"Write this down somewhere where you can see it, often—$18,000,000 is never, ever easy."

"Got it, boss. Anything else I can do?"

"Go down and check on our prisoner. Wear a mask over your face at all times. Make sure he's bound, handcuffs securely attached to the stainless-steel eye hooks, blindfolded, and gagged. Tighten his arms until you're sure he's uncomfortable. Take several photos and send them to me right away. Before you leave, stretch his arms tighter still, then, without a word, piss all over him… I'll want a close-up of that."

♦♦♦

Callie was starting to worry. Cash wasn't answering his phone. He'd been gone over three hours. She looked around again to see if he might have left his phone. Unlikely, she knew, but she was getting more anxious, and she checked again upstairs. Nothing.

Her own phone rang, Itzac, the Macher. No small talk. "Have you seen or heard from Cash?"

"No, I've been worried about him."

"I just got an email, a ransom note, and a photo. It looks like a basement room, one light bulb, no windows in the photo. He's unharmed, but blindfolded, chained to the wall and gagged."

Callie screamed, sobbing. "Oh God, oh my God…"

"Try to stay calm, I'll need all of your sharp mind, crystal clear, to help with this. I know it's a terrible shock, so take a minute to collect yourself."

Callie was still sobbing on the phone. When she could talk again, she asked, "What do they want?"

"$18,000,000."

Callie screamed again, louder, then screamed again, louder still.

The Macher could hear her, gasping for breaths, sobbing hopelessly. After a minute, he spoke firmly, "Callie, I need you. Right now. I've already called Sara, Andre, and Ed Samter, they're on their way to you. Lincoln will stand by in LA. He'll help however he can. The others will all be there in minutes. Is there anyone else we should include? Take your time."

Callie took a few harsh breaths, then said, rasping, "Abe Stein, his therapist. I'll call him now."

"Good. Glad to have you back. We'll manage this. We will. See you soon."

Callie put her head on her arms on the maple prep table. She let herself cry and cry until she could breathe again. When she was able, she called Abe Stein. She got his voicemail and said, "Cash has been kidnapped. I need to talk with you right away."

Not five minutes later, the phone rang. It was Abe Stein who said right away, "How can I help?"

"We just got the ransom email, a photo, and a demand for $18,000,000."

"Did you say $18,000,000?"

"Yes, I did. Cash's friend Itzac, who we call the Macher, got the photo and the email. He's assembled our team together, and he asked me who else could help. I suggested you."

"Good. Do they know who did it?"

"No clue."

"What can I do?"

"Our whole team, including a high-level policeman, will be here at the restaurant in minutes. I think you should come as soon as you can."

"I'll be there in fifteen minutes." Abe hung up.

◆◆◆

Twenty minutes later, at 12:30, the Macher, Andre, Detective Samter, Sara, Abe Stein, and Callie were seated around the maple prep table in Callie's kitchen. Detective Samter was saying, "We have nothing. I tried to follow the email, and it goes nowhere. We're pretty much at zero."

"I agree," the Macher said. "They want the money wired to a numbered account in a secure, impenetrable bank in Geneva, which in turn almost certainly has instructions to send it in pieces to other impenetrable banks around the world, perhaps as remote as Vietnam, Paraguay, or Hong Kong. We'll never know who it's going to."

"Was he doing anything unusual?"

"Nothing I know of," Callie offered. "The work with Dr. Stein—"

Abe interrupted. "Please call me Abe. This is not a time for formality."

"Thank you. He was doing his work with you, working hard to figure out what was bothering him, making an effort to spend time with his daughter and her family, especially his grandson. And working with Andre—" She turned to him to continue.

Andre volunteered, "We were beginning to look into the accident that killed his parents forty-two years ago. Detective Samter got us access to their remains, and we were going to begin examining them with a medical examiner tomorrow afternoon, but nothing has happened yet."

Abe stood, taking charge. "I'm violating patient confidentiality, but I'm sure Cash would approve under the circumstances. Cash has been worried about his father. Though he wasn't at all convinced of this at our last session, he considered the possibility that his father hadn't died in that accident. Further, he'd just had a dream in which his father beat him badly. Finally, he saw someone on the street several days ago who reminded him of his father. All of this is circumstantial, and literally just at the beginning of our work on this, but since we have nothing else, and the consequences are grave, I would recommend the following: Detective Samter, have them examine the remains of his father's body right away, whatever it takes."

"I can do that now, ASAP," Ed Samter picked up his phone and dialed.

Andre added, "I'll go there with our medical examiner right away."

"If there's even a possibility that the man in the car isn't Cash's father, find out where his father might have gone, what his new identity might be, what he's been doing for forty-two years. See first if you can find a new identity. Cash mentioned a cousin of his father's in Canada who might know something. He didn't have a name, but if you start with his medical records, I'm guessing whoever is following up on this can find him."

"I've got it," Andre said, then pointing at Abe and speaking to the others, "Who is this guy?"

"This guy is not just a therapist?" The Macher noted, impressed.

"He unintentionally became a gifted amateur detective. It's a long story for another time, but I know his work, and he has my absolute confidence," Samter explained.

Andre shook his head, "I should have known Cash would have a therapist who was also a crackerjack cop."

Sara nodded, stood, and then she put her hand on Abe's arm. "Thank you for your help." Then again, she was crying now, "Thank you."

Abe helped Sara sit back down. "I'll do anything I can to help."

Samter spoke up, "When we've got a name, I'll check the prisons—"

"Good idea," the Macher added. "I can help with that."

"You can help with that? How?" Samter asked.

"It's no secret. I do a very large volume of mostly legal diamond trades. Along the way, it brings me in contact with people who have been in prison or who know others in prison. I'm eighty-one years old, so I'll bet you, Lieutenant Samter, that I have more access to finding out about someone who's done time than you do."

"Point taken. Okay, I appreciate your help. If we're done for now, I'll get on finding the Canadian cousin," Samter said.

"I'm going to contact the bank in Geneva," the Macher explained. "I could use you, Lieutenant Samter, to lean on them."

"It won't work. They won't reveal anything, but I'll try to help. What are you going to tell your bank when you make a wire this size."

"I have detailed procedures established for large diamond sales. I'll follow my worked-out procedures for three different wires for three different diamond trades."

Abe stood. "I'll stand by, available, if there's anything I can do. In the meantime, I'll go over all of my notes on my sessions with Cash, see if there's anything I missed given the new developments. Please don't hesitate to call me if there's anything I can do."

"As soon as we have anything from the remains, there will be a lot to do," Andre explained. "I'll let you know as soon as I know anything."

"I'll also stand by," Callie offered.

"As will I," Sara added.

"I'm closing the restaurant until further notice," Callie went on. "I'll set up a central headquarters here in the kitchen, where we can be in touch about anything."

The Macher stood. "Those of us in town should meet here at three. Those in Tacoma, or elsewhere, should call in, then we'll all meet here again at six… Time matters; every minute counts… Make no mistake about it: we're finding Cash and bringing him home safely."

♦♦♦

Kit was smiling, in a rare, good mood. He was looking at the photo that Gus had just sent. In the photo, Cash was standing, arms stretched out. He was wet, hosed down in Gus's urine. Gus had dosed enough urine to cover him from head to toe. Kit had known that he would enjoy this photo. What he hadn't anticipated was the surge of celebratory excitement. This was the beginning of payback, vengeance, long, long overdue.

Kit gave himself credit, praising himself for his foresight in organizing this in precisely the way he had. Cash had no idea who was behind this… He had no idea that his enraged, vengeful father was still alive, capable of delivering ferocious retribution. For the first time in many years, he allowed himself to remember, to replay the beginning of this: how his spoiled, rat-ass son had started all of his problems.

He was in Tacoma then, hustling real estate. He wasn't Kit then, he was Charley, Charley Logan, and life was going his way. There was a growing market in Asia, especially Hong Kong, of people wanting to own property in and around Seattle. Charley was picking up cheap properties in bad neighborhoods in Seattle, Tacoma, and in between. His Canadian cousin, Leon, who had lived in Hong Kong and had good connections there, was here in Seattle, helping him. One of his connections was sending them buyers. Business was good. They weren't going to get rich, but they were making enough money to get by. That's when Charley got lucky.

♦♦♦

Charley and his wife, Mary, had been married when she was nineteen. Charley had been twenty-eight. He was good-looking, a smooth talker. He was always a good salesman—he could listen, he could be convincing, and he could be charming. His needs were not complicated—he liked money, he liked sex, and he wanted a pretty wife. He courted Mary, who was a country girl, naïve, but pretty and willing. Mary never had a chance. In six months, she was smitten. Two years after they were married, Terry was born. Soon after the baby was born, Charley lost his job—the security company he worked for had financial problems, and they let him go. The family badly needed money, and Charley took off when his wife's uncle offered him a well-paid job in Las Vegas. He worked security at a posh hotel there for three years, coming home to his family once a month. When Terry was five, Charley came back, taking an even better opportunity, selling real estate with his Canadian cousin Leon. He never connected with his son, who he thought was an irritating, momma's boy. Still, he and Mary worked at being together and tried to have the semblance of a family. Charley was drinking more often, and this made it more difficult. Since he was back, Charley was looking for a big score. In Vegas, he'd developed an expensive preoccupation. He'd acquired a taste for living large.

Charley's wife, Mary, worked at the port in Tacoma. She logged in whatever was in the containers coming into the port. This week, she was logging in a container from Japan, and she came upon several large cases. She opened one, then another, and she was surprised to see hundreds of new watches. She recognized that watch, the new Seiko TV watch. She'd seen an ad for one, and they were retailing for $500 each. The ad said that one of them was even in the new James Bond movie, *Octopussy*.

She didn't mention it until after Terry, their son, finished dinner. She could tell that Charley was feeling pretty good, because he'd been relatively nice to Terry. He didn't call him sissy or momma's boy. When Terry went to watch TV, she told Charley about her day, minimizing, barely mentioning, the watches.

She knew right away that even a mention was a mistake. Charley asked too many questions. He wasn't drunk, so he wasn't abusive, but she knew she had to answer his questions—Where were they? How many? Was anyone keeping an eye on them?

The next night, when she came home from work, Mary saw three cases in their storeroom in the basement. She opened one case, did the math. Charley had stolen 400 watches, $200,000 of watches. She went to their room, started to cry. She was still stewing over what to do when Charley came in. "Charley, honey, you have to give the watches back."

Charley grabbed her arms, hurting her. "That will never happen. This is our ticket to a new life. Stay out of it."

"Tomorrow, they're going to confirm everything I logged in from the container. These cases are going to be missing."

"No, you're going to change the log tonight."

"I can't do that. I won't do that."

Charley slapped her face, hard. Mary fell back onto the bed. "Stop hurting me," she cried out. "You can't keep bullying me. You can't torment our son. I'm leaving with Terry in the morning. If the cases aren't back, I'm going to tell the police."

Charley lost control. He beat her savagely, her face, her arms, her ribs, and her back. She screamed and cried until she passed out. Charley tied her up, gagged her, and left.

When he came back, an hour later, she was conscious but badly shaken. He said simply, "I've had it with your smart-mouth, disagreeable, truthfully useless fucking attitude. You belong to me. From now on, you'll do exactly as I say, and if you ever talk back, I'll beat you again, harder, longer. If you even think of crossing me, I'll take it out on our son." He waited, let that sink in. "I want the log changed tonight. Do you understand?"

"Yes."

"Do you understand? Say it."

"Yes, I understand. I'll change the log. Please don't hurt Terry."

◆◆◆

Two hours later, Mary had changed the log, and she was sitting on the bed stone-faced. She'd taken painkillers, but she was in pain, especially her face and back. She heard a knock on the door, heard Terry's voice, "Mom, may I come in?"

Mary covered herself with a blanket. "Please come back later," she said. It was too late. Terry was inside.

"Are you okay?" he asked, seeing his mom's face.

"Yes," she lied. "We fought, but we worked it out."

"Mom, this looks bad. Can I help? Do you want me to call the doctor?"

"No, honey, thank you. It looks worse than it is." She took him in her arms, a warm hug. "Let me rest and don't worry."

Terry lightly kissed her swollen cheek and left the room.

◆◆◆

Kit was getting angry, just remembering what happened next. It was the next day, and a policeman came to their door. He'd been contacted by a dean at Terry's school, and he wanted to talk with Charley and Mary Logan. Charley was working at home, and Mary called him down to the kitchen. The policeman said, "My name is Officer James Olsen. Your son was worried about your injury. Can you tell me what happened?"

Mary spoke up, "It was an accident, Officer, a fall. Terry, our boy, is a worrier, and I think he was unnecessarily concerned."

Charley added, "We're going to see her doctor this afternoon, just to be sure. And, of course, we've already asked our handyman to fix those loose steps on the stairs."

"I'm actually feeling better than I look, Officer," Mary added.

"Well, I'm glad about that. One more thing, the boy apparently overheard an argument, something about hiding cases in your basement."

"He's such a worrier. He's always been like that." Mary shook her head. "I bring home things from the Port that I'm logging in from work. I store them in the basement until I've gone through them. My husband doesn't like me to keep valuable goods overnight in our house.

That's what we were arguing about. If I'd known Terry had overheard that, I would have explained it to him. In fact, because my husband felt strongly about it, I've already brought all of those cases back to the Port."

"Can I take a look?" the officer asked.

"Of course. Charley, will you show the officer downstairs?"

Charley stood up. "Follow me." He led the officer downstairs to the basement. Downstairs, Charley turned on the light and showed the officer around the room. He opened the closet, the storage bins, everything the officer wanted to see. When the officer was satisfied that everything was in order, Charley took him back upstairs.

"Sorry to bother you," Officer James said, "I'll stop by next week to check in on you."

Charley shook his hand as he let him out.

Kit still remembered the next few minutes as though they were yesterday. In those minutes, he saw exactly what he had to do.

◆◆◆

It was 6:00. Callie, Sara, Samter, Abe, and the Macher were sitting around the maple prep table in the kitchen. They'd all called in at 3:00 and reported what they'd found, which was pretty much nothing yet, and now, they were waiting for Andre to call in. The phone rang, Callie put it on speaker. "We're all here, Andre, what have you learned?"

"The remains are mostly very old bones. They're going to run DNA tests this evening. Cash left a sample. My friend, the medical examiner, raised one question. In his medical records, Charley Logan had a broken bone in his lower left leg. The record says it happened in Las Vegas. He was working security at a hotel, and someone pushed him down the stairs. There're no broken bones in the lower left leg of the remains we uncovered."

Abe said, "That's a start. Let's assume it's not him. I'm guessing that the DNA test will confirm it."

"I agree," Samter joined in. "I've located the cousin in Canada. He lives in Vancouver. I'm going up to find him as soon as we're finished here."

Callie spoke up, "Abe, can I take a look at your notes. I know they're confidential, but I may see something that you missed."

"Can I also look through your notes?" Sara asked. "I need to do something, and I think I have a sense of how he was feeling, thinking. I may be able to help."

Abe opened his old leather briefcase, took out a notebook he'd written in, set it down in front of them. "Yes, absolutely, to both of you. Confidentiality went out the window long ago. Let's find Cash." Then, turning to the phone, "Andre, when you talk with the guy who was at the scene, ask him about Cash's mom. Ask him to detail what he noticed about her bruises."

The Macher volunteered, "I'm going to send an email to the kidnapper. I'm going to tell him that I intend to pay the ransom, in two phases, with one condition. First, I'll send half the money in two wires in several days as soon as I can raise it. Second, Cash must be seen, unharmed, before I pay the second half. When I pay it, he must be returned. I will set it up so I can hold the second wire if he isn't returned. I'm still working on that. I'm also going to tell them in no uncertain terms that the penalty for harming Cash is certain death. I know how to make that clear."

Sara started to cry again.

◆◆◆

Kit was still remembering what had happened next. If the officer hadn't said he was coming back, Charley would have killed Terry when he came home that very day from school. That spoiled little rat fuck had put everything at risk, everything, and it could have been worst (he gave himself some credit for hiding the watches in the shed). Charley had thought it through and decided he had to wait, at least long enough for this to cool down. He figured that since Mary had changed the log, he had some time before they'd find the missing watches. He'd get her to specify how much. So long as he stayed polite to the loathsome, soon-to-be-dead kid, she'd do what he asked.

The next day, Mary confirmed the delivery date. The watches were traveling by truck to New York City, leaving in six days. The truck was stopping often along the way, so between pickups and deliveries, he had four weeks. During that time, he made a special effort to be nice to the rat boy and his mom, his badly chosen wife. She was turning on him; he could sense it. Well, he'd fix that, too, soon enough.

The first thing he did was sell the watches. He had a buyer he knew in Seattle, a trader who moved questionable items, largely electronics, medicine knockoffs, and stolen jewels. He was pleased to get $100,000 up front. That would give him some support for what was coming.

After securing his new money, he worked to perfect his plan. He'd already picked out the body he wanted to use. He was a toothless, homeless man, the right age and size. Charley had chosen him in an area where many homeless people hung out. He gave him a little whiskey when he first met him, and then again several days later. When he was ready, Charley brought him to his hidey hole, a shed in the woods, and got him drunk. When he passed out, Charley suffocated him in a plastic bag, then he put him into his freezer. The next day, he meticulously worked on him. First, he dressed him in his own clothes, even his preferred shoes. He'd had another set of dentures made, and he installed them, carefully. He battered his face, then he mangled both hands, so that even in the unlikely event that they chose to get fingerprints, getting them would be virtually impossible or, at best, unreliable. Charley even put his flask, with a good-sized dose of whiskey, in his back pocket. His face would be hard to recognize, but his cousin and another reliable man who owed him big time would identify the man as definitely Charley. When he was satisfied, he put the body back in the freezer he'd stashed there. In the shed, he'd stored his car, a Ford, the one he planned to use. In the trunk of the Ford, he tied down two full cans of gas. A good fire would only help. He was ready to go.

The next day, the day he'd chosen, three and a half weeks after the officer had visited, he waited for Mary to come home after work. She was late, she explained, because she'd decided this afternoon to leave Terry with her parents. "A couple of nights for the two of us to be alone would be good," she said, smiling.

Charley almost hit her right there. Instead, he took her hand and led her upstairs to their bedroom. Inside, he sat her on the bed and then closed the door. He was so angry he could hardly speak. Tonight was the night. There was no stopping it now. Everything was set. Just so. And the dogshit, rat kid was going to miss it. He turned to her, "I wanted to have Terry here tonight," he said softly.

"Why? You'll see him in a few days." She stood, standing in front of him.

He tensed. His very careful plan was going to have to change now. The bitch had saved the rat boy's life. He looked at her, then hit her, a vicious blow with his fist. He caught her before she fell. He hissed, "You miserable bitch." In a rage, Charley pressed her up against the door, holding her neck tightly with his left hand, then hit her face and chest with his strong right, again and again. Finally, he threw her down, unconscious. Her forehead crashed sharply against a marble bedside table. Her head curved at an odd angle on the floor. Charley stared at her, confused. She was dead.

He stared at her lifeless body. Not what he'd intended. Okay, he calmly considered options. This was still manageable. Charley lifted her to the bed, covered her, then he walked through the yard, into the woods in the back, until he reached the car. First, he took the prepared body from the freezer and set it in the trunk. When he was ready, he drove the car out the dirt road and around to the house.

It was already dark, past 7:30. He went inside, went over the details again, and waited. At 9:15, he went upstairs, wrapped Mary in the blanket then carried her downstairs. He stopped on the sofa, took a final look around, then carried her to the car. When she was securely packed in the trunk, he drove off.

Charley knew exactly where he was going. He'd scouted it out and planned a course. The rest went exactly as he had planned. He drove for half an hour, then parked the car in the secluded wooded area he'd chosen. He walked out of the woods. There was a steep drop down a long rocky hill into large rocks resting below in the ocean. The drop-off was just off the road, and if he pulled the car onto the road, then angled the fall properly, it would look as if the car had skidded off the road.

Next, he lifted Mary and set her in the passenger seat up front. He attached her seat belt, made sure she was tightly in, and rested her against the car door. He smashed her forehead with a large rock, covering any sign of the cut where she'd fallen on the marble bedside table. Then, in the trunk, he poured more alcohol down the front of the drunken man's shirt. After, he carried the man in the trunk into the driver's seat, attached his seat belt, and sat him up straight. Finally, he took the gas from the trunk and poured it over the front and back floors and seats of the car. He turned the car on, released the break, and then he pushed the car out of the secluded area along the road. When he was ready, he tossed a lighted match onto the gas in the floor of the back seat. At the spot he'd chosen, there was a slight downward angle, and it was easy to push the already slightly burning car down the steep hill. As it plunged into the water, the battered car burst into flames. Charley watched, pleased. It couldn't have gone better.

He looked around. It was a dark night, and at this late time, the little road wasn't often used. Charley walked down the road, crossed over to a little dirt road. Down the road, to the side, he'd hidden another car. He started the other car, a used Mustang. After taking one last look, he drove off, to another life.

CHAPTER FOUR

Cash was distraught. They'd waited until he passed out, drenched in piss, and then pulled over a metal cot. Three men lay him down on it, then attached his handcuffs to the metal bar at the top of the cot. When he woke up again, groggy, still gagged and blindfolded, one man took off the gag, poured some water in his mouth several times, then crammed some kind of stale bread in after the water. After Cash swallowed as much as he could, he spit out the rest. Another man pulled up his gag again and tightened it.

Cash tried to rub off as much of the urine on his face as he could onto the dirty sheet on the cot. It didn't work. He simply made the area where his face was lying on the cot smell even more of urine. Giving up, Cash considered crying. He resisted that, working to understand whatever he could. He had no idea why he'd been taken. No idea who'd taken him. No clue about their intentions. No idea whatsoever where in Seattle he might be, if, in fact, he was still in Seattle. And what kind of sadistic maniac was urinating all over him, and why? He bit his lip; he understood nothing, nothing at all.

Cash tried to close his eyes. He couldn't rest. He couldn't shake the nasty wet taste, the dampness, and the unrelenting stench. He tried to think about Callie, about Sara, then about Baby Cash. If he concentrated on each of them long enough, rotating them in the same progression, he could at least breathe more normally. He did something then that he'd never done before. He said a quiet prayer, out loud, that he'd see each of them again.

◆◆◆

Samter found the house in Vancouver where Leon was living. Leon's full name was Leon Cross. He was mentioned in Charley's medical records. Before Charley married Mary, Leon had donated blood once when Charley needed it. Samter had a guy in his office who was an expert at tracking down people. Samter called this man, Marcus. Samter gave him what he knew at 2:15. By 4:45, Marcus had Leon's address in Vancouver. Samter called the chief of detectives in Vancouver, Captain Joe Colter, a man he'd worked with. He briefly told him where they were going, and what they hoped to do. Joe gave Samter his blessing and volunteered to help if they needed that. On the way to Vancouver, he got a call from Andre about the man they'd dug up. His DNA did not match Cash's DNA. Samter had what he needed.

Samter had decided not to call Leon. He knocked on the simple two-story Vancouver suburban house at 9:45. An older, tall man, perhaps seventy, opened a peephole through the door. Samter had his badge out. "Police business, Mr. Cross," he said.

"Isn't it late for a police visit? I'm old and tired. Can't we do this tomorrow?"

"Let me in, now. Now! This won't wait," Samter snapped, emphatically.

Leon opened the door, invited the policeman into his simple, modestly furnished living room. Before he could ask a question, Samter, still standing, took over, "I'm here about your cousin, Charley Logan. Lives are at stake. We need your help to find him right away."

"He died in a car accident years ago."

"Stop wasting my time. I know otherwise. I can do this quickly, the easy way, or I can arrest you now, do it more forcefully, all night, in jail. I'm a lieutenant in Seattle. I'm friends with your own captain here in Vancouver. He knows why I'm here and is standing by to help. Buddy, I'll tell you again—I'm a lieutenant from Seattle. This kind of manpower, at your house, at night—figure that out. One way or another, I'm going to get every last thing you know… So I'll give you one last chance. Let's start with his new name."

Leon sat in a chair, rubbed his neck with both hands. "If I give you everything I have, will you keep me out of jail?"

"Depends on what you did, but I can assure you that cooperating with me will make it easier for you than any other possibility." Samter nodded. "If you help me, really help me, you have my word that I'll help you if I can…"

"Okay…I'm going to trust you…give you what I know. Can I rely on you, really rely on you?" He pointed straight at Samter. "Mister…are we clear on this?"

"Clear as a bell… Now, hurry."

"Charley came to my old house in 1981. I was expecting him. I'd helped him figure out where he could cross the border illegally, and I was already working on a new identity for him. He wanted a foolproof identity, so I paid top dollar. We bought an identity of a baby who'd died in childbirth thirty years earlier. His mother also died in childbirth. No known father, no known relatives. His new name was Christopher Jackson. He shortened Christopher to the nickname Kit."

Samter was already on the phone, passing the name along, then he went on, "What happened next?"

"For the next several years, he worked for me, here in Vancouver. I ran a legit real estate operation, and he was a good salesman…"

"And?"

"He wanted more, a lot more, and finally, I arranged for him to go to Thailand, where my brother ran a business buying and selling real estate for, uh, *unconventional*, wealthy investors."

"Money laundering?" Samter asked.

"Primarily."

"We set up Kit with a good job, buying property in Thailand as a Canadian citizen. He was spending other people's questionable money."

"How did it work?"

"He had access to a designated bank account. My brother would deposit his client's illegal money into the account. Kit then bought the house as a Canadian citizen from that account. As a North American with a good backstory, he was never questioned. My brother's clients supplied lawyers and anything else he might need to close the transaction. When Kit sold the house, maybe a year later, it went into another account created for the client, and it was clean."

"Go on."

"Kit was smooth, a good talker, and he had a good backstory as a Canadian real estate businessman. One of his clients, a triad gang operating out of Hong Kong, liked Kit's work. They brought him up through their ranks, and after five or six years, he was eventually working only for them. They moved drugs, heroin made from Southeast Asian opium. Some years later, Kit was being used to investigate potential buyers, mostly on-site in the US. He was doing so well that the big boss of the triad society, Chen Li, selected him for special assignments. Kit was soon working for Chen as a detective, checking out their American partners and buyers in America."

"So Kit was rich."

"Rich enough. Living well and enjoying what good money can provide in Southeast Asia. I don't really know what happened next, but a major US distributor that Kit was checking out had been infiltrated by an informer. It was a big deal, a heroin sale for $7,000,000. As the deal went down, it was raided by the police. Everyone there, including Kit, was busted. To make matters worse, one of the cops was shot by Chen's people, and he died. Long story short, Kit was sent to prison. He caught twelve years."

"Do you know where?"

"New York, Sing Sing. He's likely out by now. I haven't seen him or heard from him, though. In fact, I haven't been in touch with him since soon after he went to prison. He had a bad, violent falling out with my brother, and I took my brother's side. We haven't talked since then. That was more than eleven years ago."

Samter was on the phone again, giving Callie the name of the prison.

After, he looked at Leon. "I believe that you lied when you identified his dead body after the accident. That's a felony."

"I know that, and I knew that you knew it too. I was straight with you. I told you all of it. I'm counting on your word."

"With any luck at all, this will never go any further. You were a genuine help. I appreciate it."

"One thing I need from you. Kit can never know that you learned this, any of it, from me."

"He won't, not from me." Samter went to the door. At the door he turned, "This conversation never happened."

♦♦♦

The Macher was on speakerphone with Samter as he drove back to Seattle. "I reached someone, a former inmate, who knew the prison. Kit had a friend inside, Gus Payton. I know Payton from several diamond deals; he's a tough customer, hard-core. If he's in this with Kit, that's bad news. I've got three of my people trying to find him. He may be in Seattle, where they grabbed Cash."

"I'll put my best men on it here in Seattle," Samter said. "Have your guys call this man." Samter gave him a name and number.

"Will do," Itzac said.

"I'll also see if my people can get a police photo of Gus." Samter went on, "Did you learn anything about the bust?"

"Yes. Chen Li was the seller. He's the boss of a very powerful Hong Kong triad. He lost $7,000,000, easy. People say he blamed Kit for the bust, and he's the type who'd hold Kit accountable. Kit's job, what he was being paid for, was to check out his buyers, protect Chen from informers, etc. I'm going to contact Chen. I know someone who dealt with him. He'll likely know how to find Kit. I don't even know if he'll talk to me. Still, I'm thinking about what I might offer him if he'll help us find Cash and Kit. That's a long shot, but I'll keep you posted… Please come to the restaurant when you're back. In the meantime, we'll be in touch with anything we learn." Itzac, the Macher, hung up, turned to the others, Andre, Callie, Sara, and Abe, who were sitting around the prep table in the kitchen.

Callie was crying. "I'm confused, and I'm very scared," and through her tears, "Why would his father kidnap him?"

Abe nodded, kind but serious, "Callie, you have reason to be scared. His father is dangerously disturbed. I believe he killed his wife, Cash's mother, and he blames Cash for having to leave Seattle. As a boy, Cash said something to a teacher at school that someone was hurting his mom. They sent a policeman to check it out. From what little I know, Charley, now Kit, had stolen something valuable from what his wife was logging in at the Port, and Cash's childlike attempt to help his mom put everything at risk. I'm telling you this not to upset you further, but because to be as helpful as I know you can be, you should know everything…and, of course, you have a right to know. He not only wants the money—both to pay Chen back and for himself—I think he could still want to hurt Cash."

Sara wiped her red, crying eyes. "Cash is very tough, but he's also worried, depressed, and upset, as you know, Abe. Our first goal, tonight, is to find him and rescue him. Andre, Itzac, what can I do?"

The Macher replied, "I share your assessment. Did you and Callie find anything from Abe's notes?"

"One thing," Sara said. "Though he didn't put it together at the time, Cash said he saw someone at First and Pine in Seattle that reminded him of his dad. Abe and Cash just attributed it to the man's Sonic hat. Callie and I both think that though he wasn't conscious of it, Cash was on to something real, not just a childhood memory, not a worrisome dream nor a fantasy. If we're right, he actually did see his dad. I'm willing to bet he did—it's who he is, as you know. If so, his dad was here, several days ago, probably to check out their setup."

"Abe, could you check the dates?"

Abe nodded. He took out his notes, wrote down the date for the Macher.

"I'll have several of my men check on all of the flights. If he was here for even one day, that makes Seattle the likely place."

Abe added, "I think Callie and Sara saw something I didn't, and I'd bet that they have this right."

"Good, good, that's helpful… In the meantime, I'm going to talk with Chen as soon as I can. I'm going to offer to pay the first half of the ransom day after tomorrow. Sara, I'm going to put you in touch with the man I talked to about the prison. I want you to wake him up and learn anything and everything you can learn about Gus. Offer to pay him $50,000 if he can help us find him. Get Andre to help. Stay in touch with Samter."

Callie called Samter back. "We've decided to try and find Cash ASAP, first priority. The Macher is calling Chen; Sara and Andre are talking again with the former inmate in the prison. Can you help right away?"

Samter replied, "I know a good New York City cop. I'll call him now. He'll know people in the prison and may be able to help us learn more about Gus and Kit. At the very least, he can talk with their parole officers. I'm on it now." He got off to make his call.

Andre took Callie's hand. "He's very smart, he's hard to kill, and he's got good friends." He turned to Abe, "Is he well enough put together now to withstand bad shit?"

Abe turned. "Truthfully, even at his worst, Cash Logan is better put together than most men I know." He took Callie's other hand.

♦♦♦

Sara and Andre had reached the Macher's contact, the former inmate. Sara began, "Mr. Thomas, my name is Sara Logan. Itzac Weinberg told me to call. I'm sorry to wake you, but we have reason to believe that Kit Jackson and Gus Payton have kidnapped a man for ransom. The kidnapped man is my father, and we think that his life is in danger. We're trying to find him ASAP. Can you tell me anything further about either of them?"

"If Kit and Gus have him, he is in danger, lady. I can only tell you that inside, those two guys stopped dead anyone who crossed them.

Everyone was afraid of them. They were dangerous, tough, and smart. Beyond that, I'm not sure how I can help you."

"One more thing to think about. Itzac said we'd pay fifty thousand dollars if you can find them."

"That's good to know. I'll think further."

"We'd appreciate that."

"Not to worry. I'm on it."

Andre jumped in, "My name is Andre, I'm a close friend of the victim. Can you tell me anything about what Gus was inside for?"

"He was an accomplished jewel thief and a first-rate safecracker. He was opening a bank safe with a partner when someone took them by surprise. His partner shot the guy, and they were caught. It was not his first conviction. That's all I heard."

"What's his partner's name, and do you know anyone else he worked with."

"The partner was inside with him. His name was Johnny Reid. He's still inside. They used to talk about a guy they called "the Cracker," some big-time bank robber."

Sara asked, "Did either of them have any connection in Seattle?"

"Gus grew up there, years ago, but that's all I know."

Sara looked at Andre, who signaled she could hang up. "Thanks for your help. Sorry to wake you," she said.

"I'll keep on it. I'll let you know if I find anything else."

"Thank you," Sara said, and she ended the call.

Andre explained, "I know a guy to call to ask about Johnny Reid and 'the Cracker.'" He picked up the phone.

◆◆◆

The Macher, Itzac, had called his friend who'd had dealings with Chen. Ten minutes later, the man called back to say that Chen was in New York City, and he was expecting Itzac's call. He gave the Macher Chen's number.

The Macher called from the bar. "Mr. Li," he said, formally. "My name is Itzac Weinberg. My friend has been kidnapped, and I've been asked to pay millions of dollars in ransom to get him back. I'm telling you this because I have reason to believe that the man who kidnapped him is Kit Jackson. I understand that this is not directly your concern. However, since much of the ransom, which I'm prepared to pay, is going to you, I think it could be mutually beneficial for you and I to talk. I have an idea I'd like to propose to you. I'd like to fly to New York City and make my proposal to you in person early tomorrow morning. Will you give me one hour of your time at 6:00 a.m. Eastern time? I know it's early, but time is of the essence. I can meet you wherever you'd like."

"Mr. Weinberg, you may call me Chen."

"Thank you, Chen. And please call me Itzac."

"Yes, Itzac, the Macher. I'm not interested in talking with you at this time. I only took your call because your reputation precedes you. When I have received my money, in full, I may consider taking another call. Though truthfully, I'm certain that even when that happens, I'll say no, yet again. I have no interest in helping you solve your problems." Chen hung up.

◆◆◆

In the kitchen, Abe was talking to Callie, trying to keep her from getting too upset. "This is a very capable group of people working nonstop at saving Cash." He touched her arm.

The phone rang, Callie took Samter's call. "I talked to my friend, the New York City cop. He was working on the night shift. He looked up Gus Payton's file. He was born in Seattle, and he still has an uncle there. Russ Payton. I'm going to see him now."

"Thanks for the update," Callie said.

Sara came back into the kitchen, sat next to Callie on the prep table. "Andre is calling a friend who knew Gus Payton, Kit's partner, in prison," she explained. "I'm still feeling useless and helpless, and though I shouldn't say this, I'm scared for my dad." She took Callie's hand.

"I get that," Callie said. "I feel that too... Abe has been trying to calm me down. It isn't working."

The Macher came into the kitchen, looking unhappy. He sat down at the prep table. "Am I interrupting?"

Callie shook her head, no.

He turned to Abe. "We found a flight in and a flight back to New York City. Kit was here, one night. I'm guessing he was here to approve the setup for the kidnapping."

"Just give me some good news."

"Sorry, all I have is bad news. Chen won't talk to me. We're back at square one, nowhere. Let's regroup."

◆◆◆

Kit was listening to Gus on the phone. Gus was asking, "What is the timing for the money?"

"He says the first half is day after tomorrow," Kit said. "He wants to see our prisoner before he pays the rest. He wants him returned once we're paid."

"We can show him bound, masked, and gagged, no problem."

"Let's set that up."

"And the return?"

"My first thought—in pieces, in a body bag."

"Nice...are you sure?"

"No, not yet. Let me think about a proper ending."

"You'll be good at that. What about Chen?"

"Once he's paid, he'll taste the shame. I have an idea about that, about how to do it."

"I knew you would, Boss. I'm already looking forward to that."

◆◆◆

Andre had reached his friend, Chris, who knew Johnny Reid and the Cracker. Chris was a retired criminal lawyer. He went too far with one of his guilty clients, and he retired rather than being disbarred. Nevertheless, he was still well-liked among his many criminal clients, and people still came to him for advice. Yes, he knew the Cracker; he'd actually represented him years ago. He'd called him, and now he was reporting back to Andre. "The Cracker talked to Gus not too long ago, maybe two weeks back. Gus was on to a big score, but he wouldn't say more about it."

"Where was he?"

"Gus was in Seattle."

"Chris, as I said when I called, one of my best friend's life is at stake. He was kidnapped in Seattle, and we think Gus could be involved. If I was trying to find Gus in Seattle, where would I look?"

"That's precisely what I asked the Cracker... He wasn't very forthcoming. He did say that he knew that Gus had an uncle in Seattle. He didn't know his name, but he said if he was looking for Gus, he'd start with the uncle. He did remember one thing—his uncle owned part of a bar, somewhere near downtown, maybe Belltown. He only remembered that because he was supposed to meet Gus at his uncle's bar once, maybe a year ago, but Gus had to cancel, and they met the following morning at a cafe. When I asked him where it was, he didn't remember. Sorry, I can't be more helpful."

"That's a start. Thanks, Chris."

◆◆◆

It was already 10:15 p.m., and everyone, except Samter, had regathered at Callie's kitchen prep table. The Macher took over, "Okay. We need to take some chances. We're losing valuable time. Chen won't help us. I'm willing to bet that Cash is in captivity in Seattle. Everything points to Gus, here hiding Cash, while my bet is that Kit made an appearance here for a day to check out the setup, and now he's calling all of the shots from New York City."

Samter's people had sent over a police file photo of Gus, and Andre spread it around. In his mug shot, Gus had a haircut and scowled. Still, the face looked sharp, smart. Everyone had a look. Even in a mug shot, Gus was distinctive.

"We have to find him, ASAP," Andre said.

Samter called in. Callie put him on the speaker. Samter whispered. "I got lucky. Russ Payton, Gus's uncle, was leaving as I came by his house. I followed him to a bar in Belltown. He's there now. It's a dive called the Double Deuce, on Second Ave. near Wall. He's a big African American fella, sitting at the far end of the bar. He wears a checkered flannel shirt and a forest green low-profile cap. Get someone here right away. I'm outside. He'll make me if I come inside."

"I'm on my way," Andre said as he stood.

"I'm going with you," Sara said. "Don't argue. You need cover, and I'm the only woman here who knows how to fight." She grabbed his arm. "Let's go."

◆◆◆

The Double Deuce was a dive, but it was also popular. The long, well-worn oak bar was sturdy enough, and it had a brass rail to put your feet on. The bar was maybe two-thirds full. Andre and Sara sat at a simple wood pub table against the wall. Sara spotted Russ Payton right away. He was big, black, older, and the simple green cap, as well as the checkered flannel shirt, were easily recognizable.

Andre ordered a beer, and Sara had the same. They talked, looking like a May-December romance. As they waited, Sara said, plainly, "I haven't thanked you for all you've done for my dad. You've been wonderful. He has amazing friends."

"There's no way you'd know this, but he's earned those friendships the hard way. When this is over, I'll tell you some remarkable stories about your dad."

"I'll look forward to that. In the meantime, don't underestimate me. If we have to fight to get him out. I'll be right beside you."

"Good to know."

Forty minutes later, Sara noted it was 11:35 p.m., Gus came in. He was recognizable from his photo. He wore a sport coat, looking snappy. He put an arm around his uncle's shoulder, then handed him an envelope. Five minutes later, he left the bar. Sara was waiting outside,

Andre came soon behind, on his phone. Gus was walking north. Andre crossed the street, got into their car. Soon after Gus opened his car, Sara got in the passenger seat of Andre's car. They watched Samter following behind Gus, at a distance. Andre followed Samter. Andre called him again on his cell phone. "Don't call in any help. When he stops, let me take care of this."

"You sure?"

"It's what I do."

Ten minutes later, Gus parked at a small, run-down, wooden-framed house. Samter had already turned off. Gus looked around. Andre, expert at this, had already pulled over out of sight. Gus went into the house. Andre was outside, watching, when the basement light went on. Sara was ready, beside him. Andre led her to the back door. His prosthetic leg stepped gently into the alley, the curved black metal attached to the thigh with perforated leather. He had a cane, though the clean geometry of his black metal leg allowed him to move quickly. At the back door, he easily picked the lock with his tools and quietly opened the door. Sara followed him, in the dark, to the basement stairs. Andre silently opened the door, then tiptoed down the stairs. Sara was right behind. At the bottom, around the corner, they could see the room where Gus and another man were forcefully feeding another man handcuffed to a cot.

Andre pointed, whispering to Sara that she should step into the shadow behind the corner, then handle the second man. He would take Gus. He creeped forward silently, then he moved with unexpected speed to hit Gus from behind with his steel cane handle, a handle that he'd designed with ultra-high carbon steel for maximum impact. Gus fell to his knees, in agony. When the second man turned, Sara stepped out to hit his face sharply with a strong right elbow, breaking his nose and smashing his face. He fell back, leaning against the wall, working to breathe, then all hell broke loose. Gus was a strong, experienced fighter. As Andre checked on Sara, Gus managed to stand, then hit Andre's neck with his powerful right fist. Andre moved skillfully to minimize the blow, striking Gus again with his black metal leg, this time smashing

Gus's private parts. The second man, even bigger than Gus, stood up, still unsteady but enraged, and moved toward Sara. He reached for Sara's arm as she expertly struck a powerfully placed kick, breaking his kneecap. He yelled as he went down again, pulling her arm, sending her flying to the ground. Andre hit the second man on his way down, sharply in the side of his head with his cane. At that moment, a gun went off, as a third man came into the room. Sara was already on her feet as she flew with a strong, well-placed palm strike into the gunman's nose and face. As he turned, Andre cracked the back of his head with his metal cane. The third man, and the gun, went down. The second man was up again. He turned to Andre, and he was simultaneously blindsided by Sara, smartly smashing his cheek with her right elbow, as Andre cracked his neck with his cane. When Sara and Andre turned to finish off Gus, he was gone.

Andre picked up the fallen gun, turned it on the two men still lying semi-conscious on the floor. With his left hand, Andre took out a case from his leather jacket pocket. Quickly, he opened the case, took out a loaded syringe, and injected a shot of Etorphine, a synthetic opioid used to tranquilize large animals, into the third man's neck. Unconsciousness was almost instantaneous. The larger man was still on the ground, in pain. Andre hit him again with the cane handle, then he injected the remains of the dose of Etorphine into his neck. When he, too, was unconscious, Andre turned to Sara.

Sara was sitting on the cot, crying, both hands touching her semi-conscious father. "He's alive," she said, happily, to Andre. "Badly dehydrated, soiled with food droppings, and soaked with urine...but my dad's okay. See if you can get some keys that will unlock these cuffs, and let's get him out of here."

Andre was already on the second man's key ring, attached to a chain. He brought the entire ring over to the cot, then, when on the third try it still didn't work, he used his lockpick and unlocked Cash's handcuffs. When Cash's hands were free, together, they helped him sit on the cot. Both of them, one on each side, helped stabilize him as Sara gave him water she found from an unopened bottle. They each used an arm around him to help him stay up.

Andre called Samter, saying, "We've got Cash. He's a mess, but okay. Get your people here. Come in the alley through the back door. Come down to the basement. We've got two of them unconscious. Gus got away. You can look for him, but I'd guess he's long gone. I'll tell you more when you get here. Have someone bring a wheelchair for Cash."

"On my way."

Cash finished his water, took Sara's hand, and, without intending it, started to cry. He wasn't screaming or crying from pain. Rather, it was a release of incredible tension, unbearable stress. Sara massaged the back of his neck as tears flowed down his face. Andre gave her a handkerchief that she used to wipe away the tears, until eventually, his tears subsided. Cash took Sara's hand and pressed it against his face. "Sara," and then, squeezing his hand, "Andre," and then he started crying again.

Sara called Callie, who put her on the speaker. "We've got him. He's fine. We'll be back in half an hour."

The cheering from Callie's maple prep table went roaring through the basement.

◆◆◆

At 1:45 a.m., Samter and two of his men carried Cash in his wheelchair up the stairs past Callie's kitchen to their apartment upstairs. Cash took a long shower, gave Callie a tender, loving kiss, then walked down with her to the kitchen. Everyone was still there, along with Alvaro and Baby Cash, who'd come to welcome them back. Sara, feeling pretty damn good, held her baby and Alvaro's hand. The Macher stood and simply said, "Welcome back."

Everyone stood and gave a long round of applause. When they were done and had sat down, Cash thanked Sara, then Andre, pointed at Samter, and sat down.

Samter stayed standing, continuing, "As you know, Gus escaped, but we have two of Gus and Kit's accomplishes in jail. Unfortunately, so long as they are at large, this isn't over. I fear they'll strike again, and we need to take precautions. I'm going to put men on Cash, Callie, Sara, and Lew. Does anyone else need or want protection?"

"Put a separate man on Baby Cash," Cash requested. "Sara will say she doesn't need it, but do it for me."

"Will do," Samter said.

Sara smiled at her dad and gave him a thumbs-up.

"Anyone, else?" Samter asked.

When no one answered, Cash simply said, "I have a long series of problems to settle now with my father, who is apparently alive. I'm going to start on that soon, and I'll need some help."

"This is an extensive, complicated conversation," the Macher said. "Can we regroup tomorrow on that?"

Cash nodded.

Callie added, "Yes, but make sure you all have time to come to a welcome home Cash festive dinner tomorrow evening at seven."

"We'll be there," the Macher answered for everyone.

Others nodded. Someone added, "Wouldn't miss that."

Cash turned to Abe. "I'd like to see you tomorrow morning. Can you find time first thing?"

"Yes, I'll come in early. I'll see you at eight," Abe said, then stood. "Good to see you back and well. I'm going home to my wife, who's wondering who this patient is."

"Bring her to dinner tomorrow. I'd like to answer her question," Callie said.

"Excellent, I will." Abe nodded to the others before he left.

The Macher continued, "In the meantime, I'm going to call Chen again. I believe I can get his attention now."

Andre nodded. "Things have picked up in that department, eh? I mean, hell, you just saved $18,000,000, and if I'm not mistaken, Chen is SOL."

"Andre, your sense of humor is hopeless."

"My good friend, Itzac, I'm doing the best I can."

Itzac, the Macher, stood up, put his hand on Andre's shoulder. "You and Sara just brought Cash home. That makes your inelegant best just fine. I'm going to sleep. Good night, all." He left, along with Samter and, finally, Andre, who also said their goodbyes.

Cash's family was left. He was carrying Baby Cash, watching Sara and Alvaro. Callie stood and put her arm around Cash. Cash smiled wide—his first prayer, ever, had worked out.

◆◆◆

It was 6:00 a.m. ET, and Kit was calling Gus in Seattle, not caring at all that he'd be waking him up. Gus had given him the bad news last night, and Kit had been so angry that, with hindsight, he was glad Gus was out of reach. He was fairly certain that if Gus had been here with him, he'd be dead now. Okay, he'd had time to think about it, and he was calmer, at least a little bit. When Gus answered the phone, plainly still asleep, all Kit said was, "You're lucky to be breathing."

"Boss, I told you last night, they have expert help, including high-level cops. I'm sorry, but there's only so much I can do…"

"Don't you ever give me that lame excuse again. Ever. Your performance after years of planning was unforgivable, hopelessly inept. If you were here, I'd cut off some body parts right now—your tongue, your nose, three or four fingers, maybe your manhood. Are you hearing this? Are you aware that I mean this?"

"Yes, sir, and I do believe you, boss. I apologize, no excuses. What can I do to make it up?"

"We have to regroup, right away. We need to raise the money before Chen's deadline. We need to decide who to take and how to get them. You need to get two more men to back you up. Can you do that today?"

"Yes, I have two good men standing by."

"Can you find another place to hide a victim?"

"Yes, I know a hunting cabin in the mountains, the Cascades. No one will ever find it."

"I have to assume that if they found you and our prisoner, the rat boy, they must know that I'm still alive."

"Boss, I think we have to assume that they know everything, absolutely everything."

"You're an unforgivable fuck up, but you're not stupid. I think they know my new name, my history, my connection with Chen, our time in prison, that I'm in New York, everything. I'd also guarantee that they've painted a bullseye on me, and unless we pay Chen, they'll recruit his help."

"They're that good."

"They will be careful, provide protection. We have to strike quickly, unexpectedly, conclusively. I will work out a distraction. I'll give you the details later today. For now, let's give them some false security. I think I'll reach out to—what do they call him?—Cash, yes Cash. I'll send an email, perhaps a fatherly remembrance."

◆◆◆

At 8:00, Cash was standing at the door in Abe's waiting room. Abe extended his hand. "Welcome back."

Cash shook his hand, "Good to be back." He went inside, straight to the red leather chair. He sat, then said, "This has got to be strange for you, too. I mean, the reality was like a dream or a fantasy or my seven-year-old nightmare. And that was before I had any idea who was behind it. I'm still confused."

Abe nodded. "Truthfully, I've never experienced anything quite like it, where your fantasized worries about a dead person turned out to be real in the present, and the dead person was alive. Raises some basic questions about what I thought and the things I said. It also gives me even more respect for your instincts. I think a considerable part of your depression, your anger, and so on, was based on real, even appropriate fears. Although how you knew those things could be out there is still a mystery to me."

"I'm somehow reassured by what you said, though I don't know how I knew those things either."

"We need to talk more about that. But first, can you tell me what it was like for you in captivity?"

"At the time, it made no sense. Who would kidnap me, urinate all over me? Who? Why? Remember, I didn't know my father was alive. I had no idea he was responsible for this. Since learning about that, it's even stranger still, surreal. He's really crazy, isn't he?"

"Crazy, sadistic, and very dangerous. You're still in danger."

"I know, and I'm worried about my daughter and my grandson. All of those crazy dreams and fantasies, that you said couldn't happen, could happen any day now."

"I'm sorry to say it, but you're absolutely right about that. I don't have to tell you to take all possible precautions."

"I will, and now that I'm free, I can do what I do best: play offense."

"What are you thinking?"

"My father killed my mother. If I hadn't been rescued, I think he would have killed me, too. He's trying to ransom $18,000,000 from one of my best friends. He may still try to hurt my family to accomplish that. I need to find him, stop him, kill him if I have to."

"If you'll forgive a genuinely concerned observation, this has become like a Greek tragedy. I want to alert you. In a Greek tragedy, the gods—fate—can play a part."

"I'm not sure what you mean."

"A father killing his wife, then threatening to kill his son, possibly killing his son's daughter, his own great-grandson. It's as if there is some form of intervention by the Greek gods. Imagine that they're punishing you, and perhaps, they're also testing you."

"Doc, I don't understand. The real live enemies are all I can handle. I don't have a clue how to take on a Greek god."

"There is no training in psychology for Greek god management. In Greek mythology, the gods rule over destiny, nature, and justice. The ancient Greeks believed that the gods control fate. If Zeus or Poseidon or Apollo has it in for you, their wrath is pretty much unstoppable. When Zeus got enraged and decided to punish Prometheus for stealing fire and giving it to mankind, he had Prometheus chained on a rock on Mount Caucasus. Every day, a vicious eagle would come and feed on his liver. Every night, his liver would regrow, and the eagle would come and eat it again the next day, for eternity. You want to stay well clear of anything like that. Moreover, so far, there's nothing I can do to help with something like that."

"Why are you telling me this?"

"The ancient Greeks believed that the gods can be generous and supportive, and also devastating and destructive to any group of humans. Above all, gods can be difficult for humans to comprehend. Therefore, mortals must respect the powers above them that cannot be controlled… Why am I telling you this? I rarely speak with a patient about Greek mythology. I don't believe in the real existence of Greek gods in the world we live in, but their importance in Greek mythology, and in plays, sends an important reminder—there are things that a person simply can't control. Remember that, and what it could mean."

"Please say more."

"Cash, in your distinctive way, I've come to see you as an emerging hero in a complicated contemporary tragedy. I believe that, and, as such, I want to warn you unmistakably about this. I want you to be mindful of unexpected events. Please be extremely careful about them. I want to help you bring an end to this horrendous tragedy that has befallen your family. I don't want anyone else in your family to be hurt, even inadvertently."

"How can we do that?"

"Your father is no Greek god. He is mortal and stoppable. I will do what I can to help you with that. But please pay attention to this—never be overconfident, be prepared for the unexpected. You don't have to believe in fate to know that there can be unpredictable results."

"I get that, but I'm not sure how to act on it. I can think about my father as a crazy, dangerous, real man. But I still need your help to understand him and make a plan, then I need to find him and stop him. Right away, before he hurts anyone else. I think he's too smart to get easily fooled, or tricked, or even bribed. My instinct is to appeal to his vanity, his grandiosity, his sense of being invincible, but after that, unless I can kill him easily, I don't have a plan. I'd like your help to figure that out."

"I'm glad, and you will have it…but for now, let's slow down. Let's take incremental, controllable steps. Why don't you meet first with the Macher and Sara, as soon as possible? Then we can talk again, later today if possible. I'd also like Sara to come to our next meeting. I'll explain why I've suggested that Sara be part of this when we meet again."

"I'll see both of them now. I'm not sure I understand where you're going. I do think that you have a sense of what I need to do, and you want to help me think through how to do it. I suspect as we work on it, it may take a different form than what I'm used to."

"Though I couldn't articulate specifics yet, what you say is certainly true. You're a very quick study, and we'll get there fast… What's best for you will have to be worked out carefully, and we'll begin talking more about all of that later today. Most importantly, we need to define your precise goals, short and long-term, and they are more complex than eliminating your father. Although you may not be aware of it, we've already begun that work, and we'll continue it later today, with Sara."

"Abe, we don't have much time."

"Yes, that's right, and I'm prepared to spend as much time as we need. For now, thank you for your confidence in me."

"It's been earned. This doesn't happen often, but I've come to rely on it." Cash touched Abe's shoulder as he left.

◆◆◆

Cash was walking back to the restaurant on First, enjoying the clear, crisp spring day. At the restaurant, he went around to the back and sat on the back steps to read an email. It came from an unknown source with no way to respond. Something in the subject, "To my son," told him he better open it.

"Hello, son,

By now, you know that I'm alive, thriving, and expecting your friend Itzac, the Macher, to pay me $18,000,000. This can be easy, the beginning of a new and satisfying relationship between father and son, **or** it can be, for you, an undreamed-of nightmare. Let's talk. I'd like to work out the details with you, and, of course, we have a lot to catch up on. I'll call you this afternoon at 3:00 PT.

Your dad."

Cash called Abe Stein, left a message. A half hour later, Abe called back.

Cash started right in, "My father sent me an email," he said, then he read it.

Abe took a moment, and then he responded, "He's wily…and I think he's playing with you. Hoping to give you some kind of false security while he runs another, as yet unknown, extortion scheme. Let's try and buy some time while we create our own plan. Don't answer the phone when he calls."

"Are you sure? I'd like to engage him, sound him out."

"I'm guessing, but I think it's a ploy, a distraction to keep you off guard. My advice is to let this one go. He'll surely contact you again, and by then, we should be further along and more able to react."

"My therapist has become my tactical advisor. How did that happen?"

"It turns out I'm pretty good at solving thorny problems. Corey, my wife, has told me, convinced me, about that."

"I have a hunch that Corey's even smarter than you are."

"Yes, and that's the first, the only, thing I've said to you today that I'm one hundred percent certain is absolutely true."

"Then I'm going to follow your advice."

"Good. Thank you, we'll talk later."

♦♦♦

Cash reached the Macher and Sara, and they both met him in Callie's kitchen. He hugged Sara, feeling lucky, and he had a hug for the Macher, who always made him feel good. Callie was out, shopping for dinner, he explained.

They sat at the maple prep table, and the Macher started right in. "I reached Chen. He's not easy, but I can guarantee you that he's very unhappy that Kit's plan hasn't worked. I straight out told him that he had two choices: Make a deal with me, and I'd still pay $8,000,000 of the $10,00,000 he was demanding. His first part of that deal would be to deliver Kit to us. Part two, which I'll explain momentarily, requires his help in recovering $7,000,000 in money that has been stolen from me. He wasn't thrilled with any of that. Then I told him his alternative—try to get the money from Kit some other way, because if he didn't take my deal—both parts—I wouldn't pay him a dime."

"Are you willing to pay Chen $8,000,000 if you don't have to," Cash asked.

"I was ready to pay more to save your life, and I'll still pay something to make this go away. But let me explain part two. There's a Hong Kong diamond trader who owes me, I'd say, just about $7,000,000. He paid me with highly skillful diamond stimulants on a $9,500,000 deal, so when I sorted it out, I actually got, say, $2,500,000. I told Chen that I would call it even if he could get me my money back, that's $7,000,000, and settle for $8,000,000 instead of $10,000,000. I told him I'd pitch in $1,000,000 for his cooperation."

Sara was just watching, mouth open. "How did he respond to that?"

"He called me a Jew devil."

"An oversized guy, with a tiny needle dick, has to be." Cash nodded.

Sara turned to Cash, mouthing, "Needle dick?"

Cash showed her a gesture with his little finger, which brought a grin.

The Macher smiled, enjoying this father and daughter. "Chen's a bonafide asshole, the real deal, but he's also greedy, and he wants his money. I think he can deliver Kit to us and recover my money. End of the day, he'll be up $8,000,000. At the end of our call, I explained to him that I knew he was the runt of a rancid litter, the seed of a rat-infested, contaminated pig, his feral mother…then we agreed to meet in New York City tonight."

"Do we have a plan for Kit?" Sara asked. "If we can get him."

"Kill him, disappear the body. Like he never existed," Cash said.

"Dad, I don't want to disappoint you, but I don't think you should kill him," Sara said, carefully.

"Why? He killed my mother. He tried to kill me. He may try to kill you and your son."

"Yes, that's all true. My instinct, my entire experience, is telling me that there's already been too much killing. It's time to end it," Sara said, eyes clear. "Now. If he thinks you plan to kill him, this tragedy will continue; even if we succeed, there will be consequences that we haven't anticipated. I don't know what, but I'm sure of that. I am."

"How can you possibly know that, Sara?"

"My whole life, I've lived in fear of me and my loved ones dying. They stole me from my mother and hid me in a horrible orphanage. When I tried to come to America, people picked me up at the airport, put me on a boat, and tried to kill me in the ocean. I escaped and found you, Cash, my dad, and then they tried to kill both of us, more than once. You would have died if I hadn't saved your life in Cuba. Three days ago, they kidnapped you, urinated all over you, and were prepared to kill you yet again. Even before I was born, your father killed your mother, my grandmother, and would have killed you if he could have. Over a year ago, enemies kidnapped Lew. Luckily, Andre saved him. Before that, people set fire to Callie's restaurant, and they killed your close friend, Doc. When, dear God, does this carnage end? Whatever we have to do—even if we have no choice but to kill him—I believe our goal, our purpose, should be more than stopping your father, an awful man. I want our goal to end this seemingly unstoppable curse in our family, where innocent people keep getting kidnapped and dying." Sara started to cry. "I didn't expect to say all of this, and maybe it's just having a new baby, but Dad, I don't want Baby Cash to grow up in this chaotic, frightening, dangerous world we're somehow caught in."

The Macher stood, put his hands on Sara's shoulder. "Cash, your daughter is wiser than you are."

Cash took Sara's hand. "I don't know how to do that—truly—but I'll think with you, work with you. I think we may have to kill him, but perhaps there's some other alternative. This doesn't feel possible to me, but, in spite of that, I think it's why Abe wanted me to talk with both of you, especially you, Sara."

The Macher nodded. "This is a very difficult, almost impossible thing to plan, harder still to execute, but what a grand outcome if you can succeed. I don't see the way, but I'll help. I can certainly cover your back while you figure out a path to follow. For now, I'll go to NYC to get Chen on board. I'll be back tomorrow, ready to hear your thoughts. Godspeed."

Cash nodded, then called Abe. He got his machine. "Abe, Cash. I talked with Sara and Itzac. I understand why you asked me to do that. Sara and I are ready to talk about what I'm sure was on your mind. Please call me with a good time."

Sara was on her own phone, calling Alvaro. "How's the love of my life?"

"You mean me, sweetheart, or your marvelous baby boy?"

"Both, of course."

"We're both good, missing you."

"Do you mind continuing to take care of Baby Cash for another few hours. Cash and I are waiting to see his therapist, Abe, and I think it's important… I'll call you after, come back to the hotel, and tell you everything, and then if the baby is down, I'll make you very happy… How did I know? Baby, are you kidding?"

◆◆◆

Abe had set up another chair in front of his desk, a traditional wooden chair for Sara. Cash was in "his" red leather chair, and he started right in, "Sara, the Macher, and I had a long conversation. The Macher is on his way to close a deal with Chen in New York City. It's got some non-related aspects, such as recovering stolen money for him, but he will pay Chen $8,000,000 of his $10,000,000 if Chen delivers Kit and helps Itzac recover his stolen $7,000,000. Itzac is adding another $1,000,000 of his own money to bring Chen's take to $8,000,000. I think Itzac, the Macher, is very generous."

"That's an understatement."

"He'll be back tomorrow and fill us in first thing in the morning. What I think you'll be even more interested in is what Sara said to me." Cash looked over to her. "Would you like to tell Abe about it?"

Sara nodded. "Basically, I told my dad that whatever we have to do to stop his father, I believe our goal, our purpose, should be larger than stopping this awful man. I want our goal to end this seemingly unstoppable curse on our family, where innocent people keep dying. Truthfully, I didn't expect to say all of this, and maybe it's just having a baby son, but I've come to understand that I don't want Baby Cash to grow up in this frightening, dangerous world we're somehow caught in."

Abe came around the desk, took Sara's hands, nodded, then said, "Bravo, Sara, bravo. I hoped you'd say something like that. I suspected from talking with you, from watching you with your child, that you'd want to find some way to protect your family, to slow down the destructive pattern, ideally, to end the tragedies. I didn't expect that you'd be able to articulate it so clearly. Because of you, we're way ahead of where I expected to be. Now, the hard work begins. How can we accomplish that?"

Cash stood, looked at both of them, radiant, intensely thoughtful. "I'm not sure I can keep up with you two... Abe, first, I've got to ask this—you sensed that she wanted that. You believed it was the right thing for me to try to do. Why didn't you just say it to me?"

"This can only work if each of us comes to believe it, genuinely believe it, on our own. After talking with her, I thought that the person who had the best chance of reaching you, maybe the only chance of making you understand and convince you, was your daughter, Sara."

"Did you talk with her about it? Prepare her?"

Sara smiled, then said, "Not really, not in so many words, no."

Cash shook his head, "What's this? Some kind of psychic clairvoyance? A shrink telepathic transmission? When this is over, we'll go out drinking, and I'll interrogate you, Abe, until you genuinely explain to me how you could possibly suppose something like that. It's more than intuition, and you had a very high level of confidence in it. Enough, the drinking will have to wait… Let's think about how to accomplish this sea change in our family. I, for one, genuinely don't have any idea."

"Start small," Abe suggested. "Let's suppose Chen can deliver your dad. What are we hoping to accomplish with him?"

"He's a horrible man, an unfeeling murderer," Sara offered. "I don't think we can change who he is."

"Imagine he's our captive, and he knows that we're able to kill him. Then remember, he's an older man, just out of jail, alone in a new, modern world. Is there any way to threaten him or anything we can offer him that might motivate him to change?" Abe asked.

Sara spoke, hesitant, "Do you think it's even possible that he might want to have a second chance, have a real relationship with his granddaughter and his great-grandson?"

"Truthfully, I think it's more likely that he'd like to kidnap both of you, ransom you for more money, and then kill you both," Cash opined, unambiguously.

Abe nodded. "I understand what Sara's saying, but certainly now, I think, sadly, Cash is right. Let's suppose we don't have to kill him, but we can put him back in prison forever or get Chen to lock him up indefinitely. With him gone, what could we do to change this dangerous trajectory?"

"What primarily do we think is causing this?" Sara asked.

"It's the right question," Cash said. "How much of it is simply my work, the Macher's work, Andre's work? Right now, I'm doing a deal with the Macher buying stolen gemstones—diamonds, rubies, sapphires, and so on."

"That's a good example of what worries me."

"All of that contributes," Abe replied. "Does it make sense to ask the Macher and Andre to join in this conversation?"

"Maybe, it can't hurt, but I think we're stuck. Even if all of us change our work, we're all going to have enemies. Sara, I sincerely would like to keep you and your family out of my never-ending crises, but unless you move very far away, I'm not sure I can."

"It's possible that we should be working together, as a group, on how to respond to crises in ways that don't escalate them," Sara suggested.

"This is a very hard group to get anyone even interested in that. For each of us, the instinct is to get ahead of the dangerous adversary, eliminate them."

"Right…and voila, there's the problem."

"What do you want us to do?" Cash asked. "Convince the evil scumbags to go into therapy or join an anger management group?"

Abe jumped in, "Cash, I know you're frustrated, but this is not helpful. Truthfully, none of us know the answer. For now, let's focus on catching Kit, stopping him from hurting anyone else. Let's include everyone tomorrow morning, after the Macher is back."

"If he calls again, I'd like to take his call. At least start a conversation."

"Are you sure you're up to that?"

"No, but I'd like to try."

"Okay. I'd suggest that you tell him you'd like to meet, just father and son, and create some kind of truce. I'd bet he'll use that. He'll think he can distract you while he comes after the money some other way. With any luck, the Macher will have him before you meet."

"I'll try suggesting that when he calls later today."

"Good luck with that," Sara said. "You can also tell him his granddaughter would like to meet him."

"That's useful. I'll suggest that, too, if I get far enough."

"All good," Abe added, then nodded, and asked, "Cash, can I change the subject? I'd like to revisit some conventional therapy issues for us."

"Yes, I'd like that, too."

Abe turned back to Sara, "Sara, I think your work is done. You were very helpful. Thank you for coming."

"Good. I'll see both of you tonight at the dinner for Cash. Abe, I'm particularly looking forward to meeting your wife."

"Thank you. Corey's looking forward to meeting all of you."

Sara smiled, nodded, and turned toward the waiting room.

They watched her leave—confident, poised, beautiful. Cash sent her a salute, right two forefingers from his right temple when she turned back at the door. She smiled and then she was gone.

Cash's phone rang, he took one look. "My very dangerous father… Is this the one?"

"What do you think?"

"Give him one more."

Cash pressed a preset note, "Sorry, I can't talk right now." He turned off the phone.

◆◆◆

Kit frowned. He didn't like at all that his dog-shit, rat-turd son wasn't taking his calls. He called Gus, who answered on the second ring. He started talking before Gus could say a word. "I want you to stake out the girlfriend's restaurant. You already know it, right?"

"Yes, boss, my guys took your son leaving from there, in the alley in the back."

"Watch it this afternoon, carefully, I'm sure they'll have cops around. Hide on the adjacent rooftops. Let me know what you find—is the back door open? Are there any large windows in the kitchen in back? How many people are there? Give me a report in an hour, then every half-hour thereafter. I have an idea. Gus, this is your chance to redeem yourself with me. Do it well, cautiously, win me over, and you may save yourself a world of hurt. One misstep, and you'll taste the shame, mercilessly."

"Yes, I'll be extra careful. Thank you, boss, for giving me a second chance."

◆◆◆

Abe turned to Cash, who was still staring at his phone. He changed the subject. "So, shifting gears, let's pick up where we left off."

"You mean my so-called neurotic disorders?"

"Your word, not mine. And given what we've learned, let's decide if—or just how much—any of it's a disorder or neurotic. I do think that though your worries seemed to be based on memories, childhood dreams, fantasies, nightmares, and so on, you also sensed something very real, something that I certainly missed. That's what I'd like to figure out. Bear in mind that it's possible, even likely, that both things were true.

"What do you mean?"

"You did have real fears, but they were somehow fed, combined with childhood memories and terrible childhood worries. For example, your childhood worry that your mother was in danger turned out to be real—she was murdered. Your nightmares about your father hurting you turned out to be real in the present—that actually happened. Your worries in the present that someone could hurt your daughter or your grandson are, in my view, now, very real things to worry about. I'd like to talk about how you could possibly have guessed that."

"I don't know. In my adult life, I've sometimes worried about horrible outcomes. It's been a strength—enough times, maybe one in four, I've been right and headed off very bad consequences."

"Did they ever accompany the symptoms you've had recently? That is to say, headaches, depression, or irrational anger?"

"Not that I'm aware of. Sure, I'd get angry or even depressed, but nothing like what's been happening recently."

"Any ideas why this is happening now?"

"When I think about that, I just think it's because it's hard for me to turn it off, forget about it, when I'm genuinely frightened about the safety of my own family, especially if I don't know why, and if I don't know what to do about it. If I worry about dropping my grandson, or if I'm afraid Sara might be taken, that's a lot worse for me than having a state-of-the-art medical import stolen. It would be impossible for me to bear if something awful happened to Sara, Baby Cash, or Callie, or Lew. Am I making sense?"

"Yes, yes, I understand that. I think having real fears about your family—especially when it's based on past history and current possibilities—are unbearable… And how are you doing now, since you were kidnapped? Do you still get the angry episodes, the depression, the headaches, and so on?"

"When I was in captivity, I was angry all of the time. I had a non-stop headache, and I was very depressed. Since I'm free, there's been nothing—until we just started talking about being nice to my dad, which gave me a headache and makes me angry."

"I understand that. That all makes sense."

"Does that mean that being kidnapped resolved my problems?"

"Not exactly, but managing the real problems successfully will likely reduce the episodes."

"C'mon, Doc, in English. Is this over?"

"Possibly, but your problems can reoccur if the right conditions present themselves."

"Such as?"

"The obvious one is if your dad threatens you or tries to harm your family."

"Yes, so for starters, I'd like to kill him, ASAP."

"Will you settle for life in prison?"

"Maybe. It would have to be foolproof."

"Truthfully, I'm beginning to think that you and your entire family will be much better with him out of the picture, forever. Moreover, I haven't really focused properly on the things you could do personally—getting the curse off your family may not be about simply changing, or somehow managing, your father, a terrible nemesis. It's more likely about something internal, something you have to change about yourself, about changing your priorities, about your orientation."

"That's a psycho mouthful… Like what?"

"Truthfully, I don't know yet. Let's have that conversation tomorrow morning with Sara, the Macher, and Andre."

"You are tenacious, no, more than that, dogged."

"I do like the tortoise more than the hare."

◆◆◆

Cash was walking back to the restaurant when the call from his father came again. He could feel his heart beating as he answered the phone. "Cash Logan," he said, tentatively. He wasn't sure what else to say when his father spoke up.

"Son, it's a pleasure to hear your voice."

Cash took a slow breath, controlling himself. "I find that hard to believe when two days ago you were torturing me and having your thug piss on me, as your kidnapped captive."

"You had some punishment due, that's true, from years ago. You had to taste the shame, but we're past that."

"I don't think you want to talk with me about punishment for what happened years ago…" Cash waited. He could hear his father breathing quickly. He had to redirect this phone call, right away, get past his father's potential fury and his own rising anger. "Let's start over. I'd like to sit down with you, see if we can come to at least a temporary cease-fire."

"That's more hospitable. A truce might be worth considering, though I do intend to get my money, $18,000,000, whatever it takes."

Cash glared, controlling himself. "That's something we have to talk about."

"Where would you like to do that?"

"I'll come to New York City. We can meet wherever you'd like."

"When?"

"I can come in two days. Day after tomorrow."

"Let me think about it. I'll give you an answer tomorrow… From here on in, I'll expect you to take my calls."

Cash stiffened; he looked daggers. "Truthfully, I've been reluctant to talk with you. I think you can understand that."

"Rat boy, you best take my calls, treat me reverentially, and pray that you don't make me mad. Now, write this down and make no mistake about it—until I get my money, you and your family are at risk."

Cash could feel the anger rising to his head, coursing through his chest, and then he was out of control. "You vile sonofabitch, if you ever touch me or my family again, I'll gut you; I'll skin you alive." He was screaming when he heard his father's thunderous laugh, followed by the unmistakable sound of the phone being smartly turned off.

CHAPTER FIVE

The restaurant was still closed, but Callie had her principal people there to organize, serve, and participate in Cash's welcome home celebration. So in addition to their usual crew—Andre, the Macher, Sara, Alvaro carrying Baby Cash, Callie, Lew with Lisa, and, of course, Cash—the others included were Samter and his new girlfriend, Kate; Abe, who'd brought his wife, Corey; Césaire, her chef; Will, the maître d; and Jill, her bartender.

Earlier, on his way in, Cash had taken Abe aside, told him, "I talked to my dad. I lost it. He warned me—threatened me—about my family, and I told him I'd skin him alive. He hung up on me."

"That was always a risk. Okay. Let's have Chen set him up right away and have the Macher take him."

"I called the Macher; the kidnapping is set for tomorrow morning."

"Good."

"Can't be too soon. I'm sorry I lost it."

"Don't be too hard on yourself. I'm impressed that you even took the call and even tried to talk with him."

"My mistake."

Abe put his hand around Cash's shoulder, walked with him back to the table. The evening was just warming up and really began when Cash came in. People stood, clapped, then sat as Callie welcomed everyone and introduced Andre, who was ready to tell the story of saving Cash.

After Andre's thrilling retelling of finding Cash, breaking in, and then vividly detailing Sara's fighting prowess in saving her dad, there was widespread applause. Cash stood up, looking much better after a good night's sleep, a very long shower, and a full day out of captivity.

He thanked everyone there for saving his life. He mentioned everyone personally who'd been part of this, with a special mention to Sara, who, he pointed out, had now saved his life twice, and Abe, who had taught him a new understanding of, and respect for, therapy. After the celebrating, the thanks, and the special mentions, they went to the buffet and helped themselves to Césaire's exceptional dinner assortment.

As they ate, Callie, who'd sat next to Corey, said to her, "I just wanted to tell you how much we've appreciated, no, relied on, your husband's help."

"From what I hear, you and I have a lot in common," Corey said.

"Besides falling in love with unusual, eccentric men?"

"Let's start right there. Abe, who's a very tough judge, thinks very highly of Cash. I shouldn't tell you this, but he especially admires how well Cash manages to be unconventional, often unconvinced with stock explanations, and at the same time, be an unexpected, excellent thinker himself. Coming from Abe, that's high praise."

"He's right about that. And I have to say that Cash and I think the world of Abe. Cash's still in therapy with him, so it's probably inappropriate for me to talk about it—"

Corey laughed. "Stop right there. With me, you never need to worry about the rules of what you can and can't do or say because of therapy."

"Okay then, you and I are going to be great friends… Cash admires how comfortably unconventional Abe is, and how perceptive, how helpful he is able to be living in that skin. You and I definitely picked men outside the mainstream."

"It's great, isn't it?"

"The best. And I definitely shouldn't say this. Hell, I can't believe that I'm going to say it. But since we're maybe just a few who can talk about it… Well, these uncommon men often make wonderful lovers, don't they?"

Corey clapped out loud, then she took Callie's hands and showed her wonderful smile. "Yes. Yes, they do."

"Let's keep this part of the conversation our secret."

"Absolutely. But let's also think of it as the beginning of a beautiful friendship."

"I, for one, hope it will be," Callie replied.

Corey raised her wine glass, "To men outside the mainstream.

Callie clicked Corey's glass with hers, then offered her own toast, "To the lucky women who understand, appreciate, and love them." She clicked glasses again.

Sara came over, quietly asking Callie, "I brought special treats for dessert. Can I go to the kitchen and heat them in the oven?"

"Of course. I'll come with you and help. I also have a few dessert specials to check on." Callie, an experienced host, looked around the table, making sure everyone was fine. She noticed that Alvaro and Baby Cash were gone. "Where's your husband and your baby?" she asked Sara.

"He was fussy. Alvaro took him for a walk. Nothing to worry about. One of Samter's policemen is following the baby."

"Good," Callie nodded, then turned back to Corey. "Excuse me, but I'm going to check something in the kitchen. I'll be right back."

Corey raised her glass at her new accomplice, then turned to Abe, sitting next to her. "You were right. This is an unlikely, gifted couple."

Abe put his hand under the table, placing it on Corey's thigh.

Corey kissed his neck, gently.

Callie led Sara around the spiral stair up to the bar, then through the back into the kitchen. In the kitchen, Césaire was in the walk-in refrigerator sorting through sausages—wild boar, venison, and elk—choosing what he needed for the second serving of his cassoulet with wild game. Callie and Sara went toward the oven, stopping at the spare refrigerator, where Callie helped Sara take out her own special pies for dessert and put them in the oven to warm up. As Sara set them in, just so, Callie left to see Césaire, who was in the walk-in refrigerator. She put her arm around Césaire in the walk-in, just as the bomb smashed the wide window and exploded. It was a high-pressure blast that sent debris and shrapnel flying, and it ignited any flammable material in the kitchen. The bomb had been propelled through the wide window facing into the alley, an improvised explosive device homemade bomb, containing ANFO, a mixture of ammonium nitrate. Sara was thrown across the room, her left leg and side punctured repeatedly with shrapnel, bleeding freely. She landed, battered and bruised, disoriented, lying like a rag doll twisted on the maple prep table spewing blood. Callie and Césaire had been thrown against the wall in the walk-in, and both of them were lying, barely conscious, on the wood floor, surrounded and covered by various marinating meats, raw fish, and shellfish.

Cash was the first to run into the room. He was in time to use his sport coat to put out a fire that was spreading to Sara's blouse. He could see the pattern of fragmentation injuries bleeding along her left leg and side. Her face was red, and she had burns on her neck and left cheek. Cash expertly applied two kitchen towels to contain her bleeding. When these two were wet and discarded, he attached two more towels with tape, firmly, to further control the bleeding. Samter, outside in back, had already called an ambulance. Abe had somehow found a blanket to cover Sara, who was holding now on to Cash with both hands, barely able to breathe. Cash whispered softly, soothing words, gently into her ear.

Lew and Andre had lifted Césaire, then Callie to a sitting position. Both of them were shaken, and Callie had a throbbing headache, but neither were badly hurt. The walls of the walk-in refrigerator had protected them from the shrapnel and other debris, though both of them needed a long shower to wash the fish smell, fish slime, and shellfish juices from oysters, shrimp, and mussels that had been sprayed over both of their bodies. Andre came in to tell Cash that the ambulance had arrived. Two medics gently placed Sara on a portable cot that they used to carry her down the back stairs to the waiting ambulance. As they put her in and began treating her obvious needs, Cash took Andre aside and told him to call the Macher. Andre replied, "I already did. He's up to speed and awaiting your call."

"Call him again. Tell him to have Chen find my father right away. Tell Itzac to bring him back, in chains, on his jet tonight—drug him, put him to sleep—whatever it takes. Tell Itzac I'll call him as soon as I can."

Cash checked on Callie and Césaire, who were being checked out by two other medics. He kissed Callie's cheek, asked her, "You okay?"

"Bad headache, but that's the worse of it. Sara?"

"Badly hurt with the shrapnel and slightly burned, but she'll be okay. I think I should go with her to the hospital."

"Yes, absolutely, and call Alvaro, who's out walking the baby. Tell him, she's okay, and he can bring the baby to the hospital, where I'll take him. I'll have Andre drive me and meet you there."

"Thanks. Will do." Cash walked over to Abe. "Did you hear what I said to Andre?"

"Yes," Abe nodded.

"I won't kill my father yet, but I will stop him. Right away."

Abe nodded again. "You're in charge now. I absolutely have confidence in your judgment. How can I help?"

"Make sure that everyone stays calm. Though Sara was hurt, none of us are going to die tonight."

"I'll do that… One last word of advice that was hard for me to understand and harder still to always remember. Please, especially at times like this, whatever you do, be ready for more unexpected events."

"Fate…" Cash softly said.

"Or Moira, in Greek mythology… Call it what you will, but yes, be respectful of that. For what it's worth, I, for one, am feeling foolish, Pollyannish, about underestimating your insane father."

"Me, too. We'll talk later." Then, an afterthought, "What the hell does Pollyannish mean?"

Cash was gone before Abe could answer.

Cash walked toward the ambulance, stopped to talk with Samter. "Damnit, Ed, you were supposed to have men covering all of us."

"I did. There were two out back. The bomb was shot from some kind of launcher set on one of the buildings across the alley. They tried to catch the shooter, but he was long gone before they put it together. The device was pretty sophisticated."

"I'm sure it was. So you know, this isn't good enough. I expect better from you."

"You're right to be angry, and I apologize. I let both men go."

"Can you get better men? If not, I'll bring in my own."

"I'll take over the protection myself. I'll rethink the team and the methodology. Again, it's my fault. There is no excuse."

Cash looked at his friend. "You're a good friend, Ed, but my daughter and wife could have died."

Cash turned away and went into the ambulance, sitting beside Sara, who held his hand.

CHAPTER SIX

Sara was sleeping fitfully. The shrapnel had been removed, a painful process, and now she had twenty-eight stitches in her left leg and along her left side. They'd given her a sedative to put her to sleep, but she was tossing and turning. Alvaro sat by her side, holding her hand. Callie stood, holding the sleeping baby in her arms, leaning against the wall beside Cash. Cash got a call and went outside.

"He's safely secured in the plane," the Macher volunteered.

"Please elaborate on what 'safely secured' means."

"Boychik, don't be nervous… It means handcuffed, a chain locked between his feet, attached to a bar under the seat, a second chain going from his handcuffs to the bar installed under his chair. He's gagged, and his head is covered by a black bag. Does that qualify as 'safely secured'?"

"Yes. Okay, thank you… Was he hard to capture?"

"Chen set the meeting, in a basement room in a warehouse. I had four armed men well hidden in the basement, waiting for him. Once he saw his situation, taking him was effortless. Why are you so worried?"

"Abe keeps telling me about unexpected consequences, unpredictable outcomes. He's been talking about 'fate' and 'Moira.' Do you know some of this mumbo jumbo?"

"I do. As a young man, I was a student of Greek mythology, an admirer of Greek tragedy. Moira is individual destiny, the will of the gods: fate. Though often impossible to know, it's an invaluable reminder of our human limitations, our inability to perfectly control outcomes."

"I should have known that you'd be a scholar of this. Why haven't we ever talked about it?"

"I'm surprised that your therapist has even taught you about it. It's not particularly useful in practical situations, like a diamond trade, except that when you understand that there are uncontrollable outcomes, over time, you learn to take extra, unexpected precautions."

"Yes, I've learned how cautious, how careful you are. I always thought it was your nature, not something learned from Greek mythology."

"I rarely think about Greek mythology anymore. Without being aware of it, though, I probably rely on the impact it had, the insights I got from it as a young man. I do have a built-in expectation that things can always go south in unusual ways, and I try not to fall apart when that happens. Truthfully, I make an effort to be ready, but it's hard to predict just what might go wrong. I did learn not to be thrown by it. In your way, you do that, too."

"To some extent, but I've never thought about it like I'm starting to. I have no idea what's coming next, but my instinct is that even if I shoot my father in the head, stone dead, on your plane, this evil sonofabitch isn't over."

"So you're right to take precautions. Do what you can to protect anyone who might be in harm's way. I know that Samter has able people covering all of your loved ones, so that's a good start. And get Abe's help; he's obviously a very capable, thoughtful man."

"Okay, and thank you, as always. What's your ETA?"

"It's now nine p.m. Seattle time. We should be on the ground before ten. I've already got a place to stash your father safely, and I have three men to keep an eye on him. Do you want to see him tonight?"

"No, Sara is badly hurt. Callie, who was also hurt, is watching her baby. Tonight, I'm going to make sure that they're all fine. Let my wretched father sweat in the dark. I'll see him tomorrow morning. Thank you again for all you've done."

"It's my pleasure. Let me know if there's anything else I can do. Should I come by the hospital tonight?"

"With any luck, Sara will be sleeping, and Callie should be at home with the baby. Let's catch up tomorrow."

"Very well. Ciao, my friend."

"Good night, my new-found Greek mythology counselor." Cash signed off, then went back into the room.

Sara was up, just barely, sitting up propped against two pillows. Alvaro was sitting beside her, looking relieved. Callie had placed Sara's sleeping baby in her arms, and Sara seemed very happy with that. "Hey, Dad," she softly said.

"Good to see you up. How are you feeling?"

Sara held Alvaro's hand. "I'm with my amazing, irresistible husband; my wonderful, beautiful child; my eccentric, startlingly smart father; and his lovely, very wise partner, what could be better?"

"Not so bad, if you put it that way... What about your twenty-eight stitches?"

"If I don't move, and if I'm properly distracted, I'm okay." She smiled, just barely.

Callie asked, "Would you like me to keep the baby tonight? That way, Alvaro can stay with you."

Alvaro nodded. "Thanks very much."

Sara was dozing off, but she managed to nod, barely.

Callie took the baby, kissed Alvaro, and headed for the door with Cash.

◆◆◆

At the restaurant, Cash and Callie walked in the back way and sat down at the maple prep table. Will and Jill had cleaned up the kitchen, but there were still scars and other markings from the shrapnel, the damage from the blast, and the subsequent fires. Callie and Cash looked around, slowly, and agreed that yes, it did look pretty much like a powerful bomb had gone off in their kitchen.

Callie handed the baby, who was waking up, to Cash, who walked him around the kitchen, cooing and talking nonsense until he rested peacefully. When he turned back to Callie, she had her head in her hands on the table, and she was crying.

"Sorry," Cash offered. "A very tough day."

"Yeah, I'm just unwinding. It was just too close for comfort."

"We were lucky." Cash put his free hand on the back of her neck, massaging her gently. "I love you, babe, more every day. This was way too close and it scares me."

She took his hand, "I need this to end soon."

"I'll be seeing my father in the morning. I'll do what I can… In the meantime, if you have the energy, I'd like to talk with you about what Abe's been trying to teach me. He believes that with someone like my lethal, uncontrollable father, we ought to be thinking about, even prepared for, unpredictable, unexpected events."

"What does that mean?"

"I'm not sure. I just don't want to be surprised again, like I was with the bomb."

"You have any ideas?"

"Not yet. At least none that are likely to work."

"Can we rely on Samter?"

"Yes, to a certain extent. But if my father got around his guys before, he can do it again, even with Samter personally involved. I love Samter, and I don't mean to be disrespectful, but I could figure out how to get around him, and my ruthless father, who respects no civilized restraints, none—he'll kill Samter's people if that's what it takes—will be better at this then me."

"That's the first compliment, albeit qualified, you've ever paid him."

"I hate to say it, but I'm sure he's an expert, state of the art, at this kind of unimaginable, malicious thing. I remember how, as a kid, I'd try to outsmart him, and he was always one step ahead of me."

"So two things—one, you're not a kid, and two, no one is better than you at this, no one. Period. So stop worrying so damn much."

"Yes, ma'am, and thank you."

"My pleasure. One suggestion—if it was me, I wouldn't think about how to stop him from doing something awful, like kidnapping someone else. I'd figure out what I could do once he did that. How I could out smart him after he'd thought he'd already won. Remember, what he wants is the money, so whatever he does, you'll have time to surprise him, especially if he thinks he's getting his money. He's not going to kill his captive before he gets paid."

"Interesting… You're ahead of me… Let's talk more about this."

"Good." Callie smiled. "You okay?"

"Just looking at you and holding my grandson, it makes me feel better. No, babe, it takes my breath away."

"I adore you," Callie said softly.

◆◆◆

Callie was still asleep when Cash kissed the baby, still sleeping in his crib, and went downstairs to make coffee. As soon as he was awake, he called the Macher. "I'd like to see my son of a bitch father this morning. Can you set that up?"

"Yes, absolutely. When?"

"I'm seeing Abe at nine a.m., so I could meet him at ten thirty. Where?

"You know the house I keep on Capitol Hill?"

"Sure."

"He's stashed in the basement."

"Okay. If you don't mind, I'd like you to be there."

"Yes, I'll be there."

◆◆◆

Abe was in the waiting room, opening his office door, when Cash arrived. He held the door open and gestured toward "Cash's chair." Abe sat behind his desk, waiting for Cash to begin. When he didn't, Abe watched him carefully, then asked, "Are you seeing your father today?"

"How did you know?"

Abe didn't answer directly, but he asked, "You're anxious, depressed, getting headaches, and so on, aren't you?"

"Yes, it all came back this morning. I even got unfairly angry at Andre, though I didn't act on it. Why does this appalling man have this awful effect on me?"

"How could it be otherwise? Your father was very frightening in your childhood, then monstrous in your dreams when you thought he was dead, and now, he's back, alive, after killing your mother and trying to kill your existing family. Of course, that has this kind of impact."

"What can I do?"

"What would you like to do?"

"Kill him, blow his brains out, today."

"And if you decide that's not a good idea, for obvious reasons, do you have any other thoughts?"

"No."

"Let me make a suggestion. Why don't you postpone meeting with him, at least until later today or tomorrow? Give yourself a chance to think through this difficult situation, and get, at least, realistic, hard-headed realistic, about it. Work on that with me. At the very least, you can take some of the self-imposed pressure off. You can always see him later, when you feel less flustered."

"That feels cowardly."

"It's not. In fact, it's self-aware, it's smart."

"How so?"

"Suppose you see him today, before you're ready. Suppose you kill him in a rage. That could end your life as you know it. Is it worth it?"

"No, of course not. But I don't know what to do, Abe. I don't want to feel this way…the helplessness…it's not who I am."

"I know, and I understand that. Once you decide not to kill him right away—and I think truthfully, that's not really an option for you, given who you are and the life you want to live—the best you can do is to have him arrested, turn him over to the police to hold him or, if they can't hold him, put him under heavy surveillance. He's maniacal, and it may not work out easily, but you don't have to feel helpless in the face of trying that."

"Any ideas?"

"Why do you want to see him at all?"

"I think there's a lot to set right, to *avenge*—starting with killing my mother, and, more recently, kidnapping me for ransom, trying to kill my daughter and my partner yesterday. The list goes on. For example, I'm sure he still intends to get the ransom, one way or another."

"Can you imagine 'setting this right' or 'avenging it,' as you put it, without killing him?"

"Truthfully, no…I might settle for life in prison in some godforsaken prison with no possible parole nor any possibility to escape."

"I can't imagine he'll want to talk with you about either of those options."

"No, it will just infuriate him."

"Do you think he needs to hear what you have to say?"

"No, he's smart, he already knows it."

"So I'm going to make a suggestion—part of it is something that I shouldn't say. Try first to use your police friends to send him to prison, forever. Set this in motion today. They can arrest them, but he'll almost certainly get out on bail quickly. If that happens, ask Samter to find a way to put him under round-the-clock surveillance. At the same time, later today—and here's the part that didn't come from me—let him know, with a message, or a telephone call if that's easier, that if he tries to hurt you or one of your loved ones again, he'll be summarily killed. My advice is not to specify how. Under no circumstances should you do that personally or ever threaten that you'll do that yourself."

"I don't think this will frighten him much or stop him from doing whatever he's planning."

"I agree, but it could buy you a day to gather yourself. In this kind of struggle, with an insane adversary, all you can do is hope for baby steps, slow him down, shift his rhythm, maybe get ahead of him."

"I think it's more likely to infuriate him, speed him up."

"Unfortunately, that's possible, and that's why you need to be ready for an unexpected attack. That preparation is your ultimate protection."

"I'm beginning to understand."

"What do you understand?"

"That he's a very dangerous man who's totally out of control. If I killed him, I'd likely end up in jail, and he's likely got his people already programed to kill my entire family. If I don't, he's still likely to strike soon, and I have to be prepared."

"I think that's a fair assessment."

"So this is only a start, but I need to start somewhere that doesn't lead to me ending up in prison. I'll talk to Detective Samter right away. I'll have him arrest my father today and have him followed if he's let go. I'll also have the Macher give him our message today. I know he'll deliver it in a way that's convincing and unmistakable. Once he's gotten that message, let him stew on it. Let's hope he takes a day to get angry before he ignores it. Then I'll face him, try to get ahead of him."

"You're smart. I won't even try to give a more optimistic assessment. Are you okay with this?"

"I think so. I'm still anxious, and my headache is bothering me intermittently. I think, though, that just slowing down, not feeling like I have to do everything perfectly, right away, is some relief. At the moment, I don't feel quite so helpless. Also, and importantly, I don't feel like I have to kill him today. No, I won't kill him today, that's a promise to you."

"Good. Thank you for that… Again, just remember what I said earlier. He's smart and extremely dangerous, so be prepared for his unforeseen retaliation. That's your best, your only endgame protection. I'd bet that no matter what you do, there's no way this will ever go exactly as you imagine."

"I've paid attention to that advice, and I've been thinking about it, working on it."

"Do you need help?"

"No, this is something I know how to do. It's still early, though, not fully worked out, and honestly, it's probably better that my therapist doesn't know the specifics."

"Yes, I'm sure you're very good at this, and thank you for keeping me from having to testify. That said, you know I'll always be there if you need me. Finally, I can't help asking, can you give me the big picture? Did I influence your thinking about this?"

"Yes, you did… Let's just say that I'm pretty sure that fate, or Moira, has a plan for me and my loved ones, and I believe that dying prematurely isn't part of it."

"Well put…you're a very capable man…godspeed."

Abe stood, came around the desk, and shook Cash's hand. Cash rose and gave Abe a heartfelt hug. Abe reciprocated.

♦♦♦

Back at the restaurant, Cash was happy to see Callie having such a good time with Baby Cash, who was on his back on a blanket, lying happily on the maple prep table. He was smiling at Callie, who was tickling him, then using kitchen utensils to make colorful noises beside his ear. Cash gave a thumbs-up to Callie, who looked at him, and then asked, "You really do like your therapist, don't you?"

"Yes, you're right. Does that surprise you?"

"With you, nothing would surprise me, but babe, this could have gone either way."

"You did talk with his wife, and you liked her, right?"

"Yes, absolutely. You know how antisocial I am, but this is a couple I'd like to get to know better."

"Isn't it against the rules for a therapist to socialize with his patients?"

"Yes, definitely, but something tells me that when this calms down, they'd make an exception for us."

"When that happens, let's find out. Now, I've got to make some calls. First, the Macher and then Samter, to put my dad in jail. Please excuse me, I'll make the calls upstairs from the bar."

"I'm taking the baby back to his mom. I'm sure she'd like that."

"Do you have one of Samter's men on you?"

"Yes, like a shadow."

"Are we clear about precautions?"

"We are, babe."

"Okay, give Sara and Alvaro my love." Cash leaned down and kissed his grandson. "See you later." He turned to leave.

"Not without a kiss," Callie said, sternly.

Cash took her in his arms and kissed her passionately. Their kiss ended, reluctantly, when Baby Cash started crying.

At the bar, Cash got the Macher right away. "I talked it through with Abe, and I'm going to cancel my visit with my sonofabitch father today. I'll tell you about it later, but in the meantime, tell me how it's going."

"I freed his mouth and eyes, let him walk around with his chains on his ankles and his hands cuffed. He's a fiend, the genuine article, with a rare foul mouth, and he's not happy. He says he wants to see you right away. He's going to be very unhappy when I tell him you won't be here today."

"That's okay," Cash said. "Two things: First, Detective Samter is going to come and arrest him today. He's my next call. Second, I have a message I'd like you to give him right after he's arrested. Please tell him, as only you can deliver it, that if he tries to hurt me or one of my loved ones again, he'll be summarily killed. Abe advised not to specify how and to keep me out of it. I'll leave how to say this in your capable hands. Will you do this for me?"

"Yes, of course."

"I'm going to call Samter now. Call me back anytime if you want to discuss this."

"Okay, but I get this. The call you'll get from me is likely later, after he hears from Samter, and then me. He's going to go crazy."

"We'll handle that."

"We always do, boychik." The Macher hung up.

Cash called Samter. "Itzac, the Macher—"

"I know who that is."

"Okay, sorry. He's holding my father captive in his place on Capitol Hill. I'd like you to arrest him on as many charges as you can. If you agree, why don't you start by charging him with killing my mother, then kidnapping me and exploding the bomb in Callie's kitchen. I'm sure you can add others. I want him to spend the rest of his life in prison."

"No problem. I'll go right away and take him back to jail. He's likely lawyered up, and we don't have indisputable proof, so he'll get out pretty quickly on bail."

"When he does, I'd like you to put him under visible surveillance, several men following him around day and night. Can you do that?"

"No problem. I'll find a way."

"Okay, then let's get this started, and please keep him in jail as long as you can."

"I'll slow it down."

"Thank you. As you can tell, he scares me, so please keep me posted."

"I share your concerns. We'll be in close touch."

◆◆◆

Callie parked the car in the hospital parking lot. She picked the baby up out of his car seat and carried him into the hospital. Samter's man followed behind her. At the entry, she stopped at the reception counter to explain her visit—bringing Sara her baby—then asked for Sara's room. The receptionist told her, explaining that it was in another building, but she could get there by following the hall she pointed toward. A doctor next to her at the counter volunteered to show Callie. He was going that way. On his white coat, his name tag said Dr. James Thompson. Callie, relieved, thanked him and asked him to lead the way. As they walked, Samter's man followed.

Several hundred yards down the hall, the doctor turned down another hall to the right. Dr. Thompson went slowly, making sure that Callie, carrying the baby, could follow easily. He asked about the man following, Callie simply said, "Police escort, they're looking out for us."

The doctor nodded. "I hope everything is okay."

"We're in good hands. It's mostly a precaution."

The doctor nodded again, saying, "Good." The doctor led them through a door into a stairwell. "Shortcut," he explained, turning down the stairs. At the landing, she saw two men, also wearing doctor's whites, nod at Dr. Thompson and continue up the stairs.

Everything else happened very fast. Callie turned at a noise to see the other two men easily subduing the follower. One held a gun to his head, the other applied a strong electric knockout stick to the back of his neck. One held him as the other handcuffed his hands behind his back. They covered his face with chloroform, then blindfolded him, gagged him, and left him in a corner, unconscious.

As this happened, Dr. Thompson put a gun to Callie's head. "Do exactly as I say." He held Callie and the baby against the wall until the other two men joined them. One of them took the baby, then they put Callie in a straitjacket and gagged her. They carried her and the baby out a side door into a waiting van, then they put Callie on a bench in the back, releasing the straitjacket so she could hold the baby. The two other men also sat, one on each side of her.

◆◆◆

It was 1:30, and Cash was on his way to the hospital to visit Sara, when the phone rang. It was the Macher.

"Samter is on his way. I told your father to expect him; I also told him you wouldn't be coming today. Then, when he started yelling unthinkable obscenities at you, I delivered your message. He actually laughed, then his tone changed, and he demanded—and that's the word he used—that you be here within the hour. He said that you should look for your girlfriend and grandson if you have any doubts about this visit. I think he's got them, and once again, he's ahead of us."

"Vile fucking devil! The bastard moves like lightning. We put personal tracking devices on Callie and the baby, anticipating something like this. I did expect something, but nothing so fast. I need to talk with Samter, right away, then I'll come back to you." Cash hung up, pulled the car to the curb, and called Ed Samter.

"Ed, they've got Callie and the baby. That means they disabled your man. I put a tracking device on Callie and a different, smaller one in the baby's blanket. They're both first-rate and use whatever cellular or Wi-Fi networks are available, plus GPS if necessary. I'll give you the tracking setup—I'm texting it now. We turned Callie's on. The baby's is the backup."

"Got it, no problem using this," Samter replied.

"Good. There's no point in trying to arrest him yet. The most important thing you can do is put your best men on finding out where they are. In the meantime, I'll have to let him go, and the Macher will promise to pay him his money. We need to find Callie and Baby Cash right away. He's capable of hurting them… I'm going to try and buy some time, at least a day. I'll call you after I see him. This one's my fault; I should have been ahead of it. I hope your man is okay."

"Makes my blood boil. I'm on it."

◆◆◆

The Macher was waiting upstairs when Cash arrived. He hugged him, then said, "I'm sure we're thinking the same thing. We'll let him go. I'll tell him I'll pay him the money, while you find your family."

"Yes, we'll have to move fast. Samter is already tracking them."

"Your father's a monster. It's going to be hard to talk with him."

"I'm sure. I promised Abe I wouldn't kill him today, that's my only guideline."

"Let's go see him." Itzac led them down the stairs to the basement.

Downstairs, Kit was seated in a chair, handcuffed and chained. He still wore a patch where his left ear was gone. He looked up when Cash came in. "Ah, rat turd…it's been a long time… I do recognize you, though, that same spoiled mama's boy with the lying, two-faced, toadying expression. Undependable, a deceiver, a dyed-in-the-wool pussy, a lifelong milksop. Always hiding behind your mama's skirts. It's a wonder that you can walk and talk without her. Nothing changes."

Cash stared at him, not responding, stone cold.

Kit went on, "I'll be giving you specific instructions. Your girlfriend and your grandson's well-being depends on your respectful, perfect completion of my requests. You can start by uncuffing me, and then releasing me. Are you following me, rat boy?"

"I promised not to kill you today, that's the only thing keeping you alive."

"You were always an asinine pest, but have you also become both pudding-headed and childishly self-destructive? Or maybe you just don't care if your girlfriend loses an eye, or your grandson has no ears. Now, turn me loose."

Cash motioned to the Macher, who released the handcuffs and then the ankle chain. "And yes, we'll even raise the money to pay you… We will pay you if, and only if, you return Callie and my grandson unharmed."

Kit stood, gradually. "I get the money before I return the hostages."

"We'll wire half the money, then the second half as the hostages are safely returned."

"That's unlikely… When?"

"The money can be wired tomorrow afternoon," the Macher said.

He stretched his arms. "You already have the wire instructions, you old money-hoarding Jew."

The Macher ignored the insult. "You are holding our loved ones, so long as they are returned safely, you will have your money."

Kit smiled, enjoying this. "A dog shit rat boy and an aging kike shylock… Now, you unnatural pansies will do exactly as I ask. I'll give you a final decision on your terms after I see the boat. In the meantime, if there's even a misstep, I'll start sending baby body parts."

"I swear on my mother's memory, if you ever hurt Callie or my grandson," Cash pointed at his father, standing up now. "My wrath, if you even touch them, will be uncontrollable."

Kit straightened his pants, adjusted his belt, then stepped toward Cash, closer. He turned away discreetly, unzipped his fly, then turned back, urinating all over him. "Taste the shame, rat turd."

Cash used all of his considerable willpower to leave without hurting his loathsome father.

◆◆◆

Upstairs, Cash jumped into a shower. When he came out, the Macher was there with clean clothes large enough for Cash to wear. Cash nodded thanks, not surprised that his friend would be prepared for a horrible, unthinkable event like this. When he was dressed, he turned to Itzac. "I'm mortified to be related to this man."

"I understand."

"Did he leave?"

"Yes, after he took my car keys. There was no way to refuse him, for obvious reasons."

"I get that. On top of everything else, we now have no idea where he is."

"Right. I think I can arrange a money transfer where he has to show up."

"Good. Let's get Callie and the baby, then make this monster disappear. I have to call Samter, and then go to the hospital and tell Alvaro what's happening. I'm hoping we don't have to tell Sara. She'll come undone."

"Yes, she's in bad enough shape already. What can I do?"

"Call Andre. Fill him in. I'll call each of them soon and tell them how they can help. Then I'll call you back and talk about next steps."

"Good, I'm on it." The Macher went into the kitchen to call, as Cash went outside to his car.

In the car, Cash found Samter. "Where are we?"

"We've got a signal, but they're moving pretty fast, going east into the Cascades. We've got men following them, but it's hard to pinpoint exactly where they are until they stop."

"Can you set up a blockade?"

"Possibly, but I'm guessing there are two or three armed men in the van in addition to the hostages. In a firefight, someone can get hurt. I'd vote for waiting until they stop and taking them then."

"Okay, you're right. I'm going to have my man Andre join you. No one is better at breaking in and getting hostages out. He'll call you soon after we get off. I'd appreciate it if you'd let him take charge of the rescue."

"I've seen him work. I'm good with that."

"Okay, keep me posted. I'm going to the hospital to tell Alvaro. I'd rather that Sara not know yet."

"I understand. So you know, they were taken from the hospital. We found our man bound and gagged, in a hospital stairwell. The kidnappers were disguised as doctors."

"Brazen sons of bitches."

"Yes. Talk soon," Samter hung up.

Cash called Andre, who picked up and started talking, "Damnit, this bastard keeps getting ahead of us. This pisses me off."

"I agree. I'd like you to lead the rescue."

"Thank you. I'd like to."

"Call Samter, he's tracking them. He knows that you'll be the boss."

"I'm on it." Andre hung up.

Cash called Alvaro. "Alvaro, I need to talk with you alone. I'm on my way to the hospital and I'll explain then. Can you meet me out front? Ten minutes."

◆◆◆

The Macher had just finished filling in Andre when his phone rang. He recognized Kit's arrogant, sneering voice right away.

"I'm expecting the wire transfer to arrive tomorrow."

"I have to sell securities to raise the money. I'm already doing that. I'll be able to send the wire tomorrow. You can confirm it by computer at one Pacific Time."

"I will come back to the specifics. But first, I have another demand; it's nonnegotiable. I'll want a yacht, at least forty feet long. It must sleep four comfortably and be able to travel long distances at twenty knots or more. It must be well equipped and well stocked for travel. I'll want that by noon tomorrow. I will not release the captives until I've confirmed the wire and have been safely at sea for twenty-four hours."

"I can't find that by noon tomorrow."

"No, you will find it, exactly as I specified, or you and the rat turd will receive the baby's ears and several fingers. Also, the woman's nose or eye or both. I will not tolerate disobedience or the slightest deviation from my specified demands."

The Macher cringed. "I'll figure out a way."

"One more essential, call it an imperative. Regarding the wire, it has to be for the full amount, all $8,000,000. Anything less will result in the same grave consequences I just detailed. I will release the captives unharmed, if you meet those demands. Text me with the pick-up place for the boat. I'll expect to be aboard, traveling with my crew at twelve thirty tomorrow. As I said, when I've confirmed the wire and have been safely at sea for twenty-four hours, I'll release the woman and the baby. I'll tell you where when I have the money."

"You're not only malicious, you're shamelessly untrustworthy."

"Shut up, Jew scum, don't aggravate me, or in a heartbeat, you'll be an old kike tasting excruciating shame. You have work to do. Get on it." Kit hung up.

♦♦♦

Kit called Gus next. "Give me an update," he ordered.

"All is well, boss. We're arriving at the hideout momentarily. No one has followed us. The cabin is isolated, as you know, and inaccessible without detailed directions. The hostages are safe, and the woman is terrified, as she should be."

"Good. Here's the plan. They'll be delivering a fast, well-equipped yacht to me by noon tomorrow. They'll be wiring all—I repeat—*all* of our money, $8,000,000, soon after. Once I'm aboard and at sea, I'll confirm that the wire has arrived. That should happen at one fifteen. I'll call you no later than one thirty. If all has gone as it should, I'll want you to kill the hostages, bury them somewhere remote, difficult to find, in the woods. You can then pay and release your crew, then drive to Everett, where I'll pick you up. I have another boat. I stashed it in Everett when we first made our plan. We'll switch to that boat and leave for Canada. I'll let them search for the hostages. I told them we'd release them twenty-four hours after I'm safely at sea. If you're clever, they'll never find them."

Gus turned away so Callie couldn't hear this. "The baby?"

"Do I have to tell you everything twice?"

Gus turned back. "No sir, boss."

"Text me tonight, at nine, that all is well, then tomorrow morning at ten, the same thing. Use a code—let's say Sing Sing for old time's sake."

Gus repeated, "Nice touch. Sing Sing, nine p.m. tonight, ten a.m. tomorrow. Will do."

◆◆◆

The Macher reached Cash as he was near the hospital. Cash pulled over to park while he took the call.

"It's more complicated and riskier than I expected. Your father wants us to get him a large boat, capable of traveling long distances, at good speeds, by noon tomorrow. Further, he wants us to pay all the money, $8,000,000, tomorrow. He's threatened sending body parts from Callie and Young Cash if we don't comply. I figure the boat is our best option. I'll find him something, rent it if I have to, and you can confront him onboard or nearby, wherever I meet him."

"We're thinking the same thing. Samter can get you a boat if you need his help."

"Good to know. I do know a guy who sells and rents. I'm pretty sure he'll fix me up.

"First, we have to rescue the captives."

"Exactly."

"If we don't, he'll kill them."

"Yes, he will."

◆◆◆

Alvaro was pacing in the parking lot when Cash pulled in. Cash got out, pointed that he'd meet Alvaro at a nearby bench. When Cash sat beside him, he started right in, "Alvaro, there's no easy way to explain this, so just listen and bear with me. Both Callie and your son have been kidnapped." Cash took his arm. "As far as we know, they're both okay."

Alvaro put his head in his hands, fighting back tears.

Cash put his arm around him. "They're both wearing hidden trackers, and Samter and Andre have men following them. We're going to free them as soon as they stop. We should be able to do that sometime this evening. This is up to you, but I think it's better if Sara doesn't know until we get them back."

Alvaro took Cash's arm; he was crying now. "How is this possible? My God, how could you let this happen?"

"From what little we know, they took them here, from the hospital. Callie was bringing the baby back to you and Sara. She had a police bodyguard. There were three experienced attackers. According to Samter's man, they were dressed as doctors. I didn't expect anything so soon. There's no excuse. It's my fault. Should we tell Sara? Finally, this is your decision."

"Absolutely not. You know her, and there's no one stronger, but if you tell her that her baby has been kidnapped, she'll be beside herself, hysterical… Help me decide what to say, but I can't tell her someone has stolen our baby."

"I understand, believe me. I know how hard this must be for you. You're a good man, Alvaro. Thank you for sparing her from this."

Alvaro stood, crying again. Cash stood beside him, held him in his arms. "We're going to bring them back. I promise you that."

Alvaro held Cash, silent.

"Alvaro, we'll tell her when we bring him and Callie home. I have to leave now, to help in the rescue. I'll let you know as soon as I know anything. In the meantime, tell Sara that Callie took the baby for the day so you and she wouldn't have to worry about him. Tell her she talked with you, and she'll call in after dinner time."

Alvaro stepped back, faced Cash's eyes. "Bring them back, Cash. For Sara, for me, for Lew, and for you. This is more important than anything you've ever done."

"I know, and I will." Cash hugged him, fiercely, then he left.

♦♦♦

In the car, Cash called Abe, who picked right up.

"They kidnapped Callie and my grandson."

"Oh dear God, your worst nightmare. Were you prepared?"

"I hid trackers on both of them, so we're following them. We hope to rescue them when they stop."

"Good... Smart... Did you see your father?"

"I had to. He insulted me and the Macher harshly, vilely, then he urinated on me. If I hadn't promised you, I would have killed him."

"He's an animal, and he deserves to die, but thank you for keeping your promise. That was important. Do you know where he is?"

"He took the Macher's car and took off. We have no idea where he is. He changed the deal. He wants an expensive boat set up for long-distance travel by noon tomorrow. He also wants all of the money, right away. If he gets it, I think he'll kill the hostages. Our best chance is to get Callie and Baby Cash, then I'll take him at the boat. He'll believe that he's safe because he won't know that we have the hostages."

"Find your family, then call me as soon as you can after you get them home safely."

"With any luck at all, we should have Callie and my grandson back tonight, tomorrow, latest."

"Please keep me posted if it happens tonight. Cash, my hopes, and my heart, are with you."

"Thank you. I'll let you know."

♦♦♦

Cash and the Macher met at Samter's office at 6:30. There was a large map on the wall and a line drawn on the map that tracked their progress. Cash could see that they'd gone over Snoqualmie Pass and had turned off into sparsely inhabited wooded country before Easton. Andre was with the followers, and Cash got Andre on the phone. He put him on the speaker.

"It looks like they stopped at some kind of cabin in the woods. We've gathered nearby. It's already dark, and we're ready to move on them. Do we have your go-ahead?"

Samter looked at Cash, who nodded. "You do," Samter said.

◆◆◆

Andre and three Seattle policemen in plainclothes moved quietly through the woods until they could see the cabin. They were still hidden in the woods. They could see that the cabin was lit, but it was too far to see how many people were inside. Andre could see that the car wasn't outside. There was a shed behind the cabin, and he assumed that the car was hidden in that shed. Andre signaled to the senior policeman, Sergeant Kelly, to move in closer to take a look inside the cabin.

The sergeant, clearly experienced at this, crept around the trees until he reached the closest side of the cabin with a window. He crawled on his belly across the grass until he was under the window. He stood slowly, carefully. Looking inside, he saw nothing. He inched to another window, peering inside. He could see that the light was on, but he saw no one inside. He snuck around the corner of the cabin to a window near the front door. Looking in again, he saw no signs of life. He crouched, raised a cell phone, and signaled Andre.

"It looks like there's no one here," he whispered. "Bring the others to back me up, and I'll go inside."

"On our way," Andre replied. He signaled for another man to follow him, and they took positions on the ground outside where they could cover the sergeant at the front door.

The front door was unlocked, and Sergeant Kelly opened it quickly, falling to his knee inside with his gun drawn. He looked around, then stood up. Inside, he could see where one of the tracking decoys was resting on a chair. He waved for the others to come in. When they came inside, he pointed to the tracking device. "We were set up. They found the device, planted it here some time ago, to draw us in, then left."

Andre picked up the device, then called Cash. "They left a device here, but they're long gone. We've been had."

"Which device is it."

Andre took a photo of it with his phone and sent it to Cash.

"That's Callie's device. The smaller one is hidden in the baby's blanket. I'll put Samter on, and he can give you the info. I hope Callie turned it on."

Cash gave the phone to Samter. He turned back to the Macher. "They know we were following them. I hope they can't pick up the second signal. It's—"

Samter interrupted, "We're not getting the second signal. Nothing."

"Damnit," Cash said loudly, then, "God fucking damnit!"

◆◆◆

Callie was in the back of the van, holding the baby in her arms. The baby was crying, unhappy with the new place and the new people. "Can I walk him around," Callie asked one of the men, Gus actually, who she thought she recognized from Lincoln's photo.

"Sure, just make him shut up."

"Why don't you shut up, you idiot," she thought to herself as she walked around the tiny area in the back of the van. About the third time around her tiny circle, Baby Cash started to scream. Callie recognized the sound, and the smell that indicated he needed to be changed. She called over to Gus, who was clearly in charge, "Can you ask the driver to pull over. I need a minute to set him down outside, so I can change his diaper. I have spare diapers in my bag." She pointed to the bag she'd had when they took her.

Gus said something to the driver, who pulled off the road into a pull-off area where they could stop. Callie got off and set the baby on his back on his blanket, which she'd spread on the grass. Two of her kidnappers followed. One man stood on each side of her. She removed his dirty diaper, set it on the corner of the blanket, then took a new diaper from her bag. She cleaned up his bottom with a wipe. As she put that wipe beside the dirty diaper, she reached her hand under the corner of the blanket underneath. The tiny second decoy was tucked inside a small case she'd made in the corner of the blanket. She checked, and the men, uncomfortable with watching her changing the dirty diaper, were looking elsewhere. With one hand, she moved the new diaper just below the baby's bottom, with her other hand in the case, she turned on the second decoy.

When she'd changed the diaper, she dropped the dirty diaper and the wipe into a plastic bag, then picked up the baby in his blanket. "Find a place to throw this away," Callie said as she gave the plastic bag to one of the men, who took it reluctantly.

Without drawing attention, she went, escorted by the two guards, back into the van.

◆◆◆

At Samter's office, Cash, Samter, and the Macher were worried. Samter had turned on the tracker for the second decoy, and it wasn't sending a signal. Cash was on the phone with Andre, who couldn't follow their car without a tracking signal. "I have no idea where they went," Andre was saying.

"If we lose them, we may never get them back," Cash announced, beside himself.

"We won't let that happen," Andre replied.

"How?"

"We can take three or four cars and try to locate them, but we don't even know what their car or cars look like."

"That's not going to work—"

Samter interrupted, "Hold on…maybe…okay…yes…yes! We got a signal. We're back in business. They're back on the highway, and the baby's decoy is sending a signal."

Andre yelled out loud, then, after a beat, "We're off," he exclaimed. "Give us the signal and the coordinates and we'll find them."

The Macher turned to his friend. "Cash, you can take a breath. You have the best possible people on this, and the kidnappers have no idea about the second device. It's our turn now."

Cash sighed, relieved. "Let's get my family back tonight."

CHAPTER SEVEN

They'd retraced their route, and now Gus directed the driver to go off the road just before Snoqualmie Pass. After several miles, he pointed out an unpaved road that turned into the forest. They were soon in a remote area. He took the unpaved road for several more miles, then Gus pointed out an unused, unpaved, abandoned road. They slowly followed that road until they arrived at a small, empty cabin. It was a cabin Gus knew because he'd been there hunting with his uncle. His uncle owned it and used it regularly during the hunting season. This time of year, it was never used.

They parked near the cabin, and Gus found the key under a large rock nearby, where his uncle kept it hidden. He used the key to unlock the door. Inside, it was dark and dusty. He turned on the light. It was small, with one main room for kitchen and living room, two small bedrooms off the living room. He put Callie and the baby in the near bedroom, locking the door from the outside.

Callie found the small light. Luckily, the baby was sleeping, and she lay him down on his blanket on top of the musty bedcover. Callie sat beside him on the bed. She cried softly, worn down with hiding her fears about these men, keeping the baby unharmed, and making sure no one suspected the transmitter in his blanket. She was especially frightened because she'd heard bits and pieces of Gus's call with Kit, and she was pretty sure that they planned to kill both her and the baby. She carefully removed the device from the baby's blanket. She pressed the SOS button designed primarily to be used by a child, for example, to send an emergency signal to the tracker.

◆◆◆

Andre had already pinpointed the area of the cabin in the woods. When he got the SOS signal, it pinned it down more precisely. It wasn't far, and he guessed that they were there for the night. They pulled off the side of the road just before the abandoned road, to wait for Samter and Cash. While the others waited, Andre hiked through the woods to scout out the cabin. He could see it, lit up, with the van out front. He used night vision binoculars to see what he could through the windows. He made a large circle through the woods around the cabin. He saw a back door.

Cash and Samter were driving fast toward the area where Andre had located the hostages. They pulled off the road beside Andre's car to make a plan. In Andre's car, two of Samter's best men were waiting. Andre emerged from his scouting expedition just after they arrived.

They gathered outside the car. It went without saying that Andre was in charge.

"There are three of them. Gus and two I don't know. I didn't see Callie and the baby, but from the back, I could see where one of the bedrooms was lit up. It was a small window, too small for her to get out, but I'm betting that Callie and the baby are locked in that bedroom, out of the line of fire, which is good for us. There's also a back door, near her room. Cash, I know what our objective is, and I know that we can't allow either of the hostages to be hurt—"

Samter jumped in. "It's possible that unless we succeed, they plan on killing the hostages." He went on, sure of himself. "There's too much at stake to take a risk. If we have to, we should kill all three of them, then free the hostages."

Cash added. "If they get a chance to get into the bedroom, they'll put a gun to Callie's head and then take her and the baby to make us let them go."

Andre closed the deal. "We all agree. I'll take Gus. Samter, you and Sargent Kelly each take one of the others. If one of them surrenders, we can take him alive. Otherwise, kill them, or wound them so they can't defend themselves. Cash, you're back up in the unlikely event that one of us misses or gets hit. We have two battering rams. One will explode a disorienting blast when it opens the door. One of our policemen, Jack, Andre pointed, will use the explosive ram on the front door. He will open it, then drop to the ground on the side. Sargent Kelly and Samter will come through immediately firing. Al, our second policeman, will simultaneously use a standard battering ram on the back door, then drop to the ground. Cash and I will come through the open back door. I'll be firing at Gus. Cash, fire at anyone still standing. After the initial blast, Cash, your objective is to keep anyone from opening the bedroom door, which will be to your left coming in. Before we separate, I'll designate a specific time for entry. When we get to our respective doors, undetected, at that time we all go, with everything we've got. Let's get our equipment and go."

Ten minutes later, Andre had led all of them to a spot in the woods where they could see the cabin but couldn't be seen. He set a designated time, in precisely twelve minutes, then took Al and Cash through the woods around to the back. It was dark, and with two minutes to spare, both groups expertly sneaked, inched, and crawled to each respective door.

At precisely the designated time, all hell broke loose. The front door blasted open, sending a disorienting burst of smoke and spattered gunpowder, followed instantly by two armed men, firing. Simultaneously, the back door flew open, with two other men firing expertly. In less than a minute, all three men inside were down. Two were severely disabled, shot two or three times each in the chest and legs. Gus was dead.

Cash had gone directly to the locked bedroom, opening it, then closing it behind him. Inside, he had Callie in one arm and Baby Cash in the other. He was uncharacteristically crying. Callie, too, was crying loudly. The baby watched both of them, curious. When the crying subsided, Callie said, "My sweet, remarkable love, I was waiting for you."

"Are you and the baby okay? Unhurt?"

Callie kissed him. "Yes, yes, though this was an ordeal."

"I'm sure, and I'm so sorry you and the baby had to go through it."

"Your grandson was great. He's like you already."

"I need to call Alvaro, right away."

"Yes, and I need to give you the code they were using to contact your father."

"Okay, after the call. Thank you," Cash said, as he was calling Alvaro. Alvaro picked up on the first ring. Cash spoke up right away, "Everyone is fine. All is well. You can tell Sara we'll be on our way to you shortly."

"Thank God, and thank you, Cash. You've saved our lives, too."

"I know that Sara is going to be really angry. Don't let her take it out on you. Tell her that I made you keep it a secret; tell her whatever you want. I'll tell her everything when we get there. It's my fault. She was right about how this is just too dangerous. I'm responsible, I'm to blame. I'll see you soon."

"Don't be too hard on yourself."

"Not to worry, Sara will take care of that."

Callie looked at him. "You're a good man, a great man, and an outstanding lover and partner, but get ready. Telling Sara about this is going to be worse than our worse fights, early on. You remember how angry I got when you smuggled those erotic netsuke into my restaurant?"

"Yes, you called the police, who arrested me, and then famously said, and I quote, 'When you get out of jail, don't ever come back here.'"

"Yes, exactly. Well, honey, that was nothing, just a trifle, compared to what Sara is going to feel about you putting her new baby's life at risk."

"It could have been much worse."

"Yes, I understand, but she's still going to be upset and angry—livid, in fact."

"One crisis at a time, honey. Please. I love you and my grandson, so much that I'll somehow survive my daughter's wrath."

"I love you like that, too. Let's bring her son home, right away."

Cash kissed her again, then took both of them into the living room.

In the living room, there were hugs, and expressions of relief, all around. The dead body had already been covered; the severely wounded others were crudely bandaged, handcuffed, and gagged. Both of Samter's policemen had gone to bring back cars. Everyone agreed that the first job was to bring Callie and Baby Cash home.

Callie interrupted to repeat what she'd said to Cash, "I overheard a call between Gus and Kit. Kit wanted to get a simple text—all is well—sent at nine tonight, then another at ten tomorrow morning. The code name, not surprisingly, is Sing Sing. I'm sure that the first one has already been sent, but you should send the second one in the morning."

Samter said, "I have Gus's phone. We can send it from there."

"Will you take care of that?" Cash asked.

"No problem, this should be quick and simple. I'll write it out, then text it to you before I send it."

"Thanks."

Andre led Cash and his family members to his car. He helped them in the car, and then they were off. The others prepared to deliver the captives under guard to the hospital and bring the dead body to the morgue.

In the car, Cash had another call to make. "Itzac," he said when the Macher picked right up.

"We're good. Better than good. I'm in the car with Callie and the baby, Andre is driving. Everyone is fine. No injuries among our group. Two of the kidnappers are wounded and captured. Gus, the third, is dead. I'll give you the details tomorrow."

"Thank you for the update. Well done."

"As you said, it was our turn. I'll call you tomorrow."

"Good, talk then."

"One more call," he said to Callie.

"Let me guess…your therapist, Abe."

"How did you know?"

"Hon, how could I not know that?"

Cash dialed. Abe picked up. "All is well," Cash explained. "Callie and my grandson are with me in the car going home."

"Bravo. You're a very capable man. Don't ever forget that."

"I'm not feeling so capable at the moment. My next job is to bring my grandson home, and explain to his mother, my daughter—who said, in your presence, that this was too dangerous, that it had to stop—she's going to be very upset and absolutely furious."

"Maybe, and you'll deal with that, but she'll also be thrilled that her son is fine, and that her son's grandfather takes such good care of his family."

"Abe, you know how much I like you, but let your new friend give you some free, good advice—do not, under any circumstances, bet any of your own money on this well-intentioned but half-baked, over-optimistic shrink idea that you just confidently volunteered."

"I see. Okay, I'm sorry, and I won't… Where do things stand with your father?"

"He doesn't know that his hostages have been freed. I'm going to see him tomorrow. He's picking up a boat that we're providing. One way or another, I'm going to end this, take him down and out forever."

"Do you want to talk about that?"

"Not really. I know where you stand. I've thought about it, and I'm not sure that I see it the same way."

"It's your decision, and truthfully, I don't think you need my help. You've heard my concerns, even Greek mythology. You've thought about those things and now it's up to you."

"I didn't expect that…"

"Go slay the dragon, lay it to rest… Don't overthink it. Rely on your instincts. You're not going to kill him unless you have no choice…it's time to move on."

"Thank you for that."

♦♦♦

It was 11:30 p.m. when Cash, Callie, and the baby arrived at the little house that Sara and Alvaro had rented. They were both on the porch, waiting. Sara was wearing a robe over her nightgown. They could see how she leaned against the porch rail to support her wounded left side, which was still covered with stitches and, in some places, visibly bandaged. Callie went first up the stairs, holding the baby. Sara literally swooped down, taking the baby in her right arm. She held him close, crying softly. Cash followed up the stairs and approached Sara, who turned away. Cash said, "I'm sorry. I don't have the right words, but I'm so sorry. We took precautions, but I just wasn't careful enough. I should have been ahead of it."

Sara turned back, her eyes blazing, "How could you possibly ever, ever, let this happen? Since Alvaro told me about it this evening, it's all I've been able to think about. You almost lost our baby, Dad... you almost lost Callie..." She stuck out her left thumb and forefinger, holding them as close together as possible without touching. It made her wince. "It was this close," she grimly said. She started crying again. "I'm sorry, but I can't live in your world. I can't be with you. You can't be with your grandson. It's just too dangerous. We're going back to Miami, even Cuba, if we have to, and we just can't be connected with you. I love you, and it breaks my heart, but the cost of having you in our family is just too high."

"Sara, we have to find another way. I desperately want, I need, you and my grandson and Alvaro in my life."

"I've been keeping it together, being polite, civil with my dad, but shit, god fucking damnit, unless you remake—no, totally reinvent—your way of life, you're going to kill my child," she cried out, despairing.

"Honey, I won't ever let that happen."

"How? It almost happened today? Listen to what I'm telling you."

"I'm trying, but reinvent my way of life—what does that mean?"

"It means exactly what it says—you have to do whatever it takes, no matter how difficult it is, to stop putting your family and your loved ones in mortal danger. You have to do that reliably, ALL OF THE TIME! Truthfully, I don't think you want to make that kind of change, and even if you did, I don't think you could."

"Please, will you wait? Hang on and let me try?"

"Hell, no! We already did that," she said, really frustrated now. She held her baby close with her right arm while she leaned on the porch rail with her left. "Do you remember what I said back in your therapist's office?"

"…more or less."

"Well, here it is again, exactly, 'I want our goal to end this seemingly unstoppable curse on our family, where innocent people keep dying… I don't want Baby Cash to grow up in this frightening, dangerous world we're somehow caught in…' Did you think I didn't mean that? Do you think that because you're smart and charming, you can do whatever the hell you want to do? Well, mister, those days are over with my little family. Unless and until you change your life—no, your way of life. Unless and until you're not putting yourself and your loved ones in danger…and I mean NEVER, EVER… Unless and until you can do that, I want you to stay the fuck away from us. Period." She was dead serious and visibly upset. Her eyes were glaring.

"Sara, please slow down. Yes, I can try, but do you expect me to give up my entire way of life, who I am?"

"That's precisely what you have to do—precisely—if you ever want to be part of Baby Cash, Alvaro, and my little family again. And it's not enough to just make the effort. You have to actually do it. You have to prove that you've done it."

"Can I think about this? Can we talk about it again?"

She paused, took a breath, exasperated. "As it stands, it's a waste of time to talk about this again. What we're on right now, is a very fast train, an unstoppable, runaway train that will kill more of our family and close friends. Again and again. Next time it could be Lew or Alvaro, it could be the Macher or Andre. I'm about to get off of this train. We have to go far away from you to even have a chance to be able to really, truly get off. But there's no middle ground. Unless *you* can somehow get off—genuinely get off, forever—we'll never have a chance. It's all or nothing. I don't think you can do it. Unless, and until, you can, unmistakably, we have nothing to talk about." Sara looked at her dad, sadly, then took the baby into the house.

Callie took Cash's arm. "Sorry," she said.

"Even worse than you predicted, and her mind is made up."

"Yes, all true. It's uncanny to me, how much she's like you. She thinks about it, but once she's clear, her mind is made up and she's set, determined."

"Yes, I do recognize that…I know this was hard for her, too…"

"Very."

"I do admire her. She's a strong, wonderful woman."

"Yes, she is. You have a very hard decision to make if you want to have a life with her and her family."

"I know that. Please do me one very big favor. I have to deal with my father tomorrow. It's very important, and however it goes, it's going to be very intense. Please ask Sara to give me at least another day to take care of that, and then another day to try and figure out how I can work it out with her. You can tell her that I heard her, and I don't think she's wrong. I'm not going to try and change her mind. It's just that I don't have any idea whatsoever what to do, and I need some time to think. Will you talk with her?"

"Of course, sweetheart. No promises, but I think I can get you some time."

"Thank you, that would help."

Callie took his arm and walked him down to Andre's car. Inside, Andre asked, "I was watching all of your faces. That didn't go too well, eh?"

"Let it go, Andre," Callie gently suggested. "Just let it go."

◆◆◆

In the morning, after pouring his coffee, Cash called Abe. "Can you see me this morning?"

"I have a meeting I can reschedule. Can you be here in twenty minutes?"

"Yes. On my way."

Twenty minutes later, Cash was in the now familiar red chair opposite Abe. "I was up most of the night. Sara and her family are leaving, far away, if Miami isn't enough, perhaps as far as Cuba, unless I change my way of life—totally. Never put my loved ones in danger like they've been again. You've heard her talk about this."

Abe nodded. "Yes."

"Sara's decision—and her mind is made up—made me think about my own father."

"I can understand that."

"Sara thinks she needs to be disconnected from me for her family to be safe."

"Is that familiar?"

"In a way. I mean, I know I'm not at all like my father, but the outcome—that she can't safely live with me—is not only upsetting, it's unnervingly familiar."

"Yes, but whatever you decide to do with Sara, you'll never, ever be like your father."

"Thank you, and truthfully, I do know that. What it made me understand, though, what it made me want to do, is change this family curse. I want Sara and her family to be able to live safely near me, to comfortably spend lots of time with me."

"I think you need to separate two things. You're seeing your father later today. That's a very important moment in your life. I believe you're absolutely right—you have to stop your father. Period…it's going to be hard. He is, at the end of the day, still your father. I think, though, that you're ready to do that… I think, however, to change, as you call it, your family curse, is another matter entirely. Sara is right about that. You have to change your way of life, dramatically. It's not finding a middle ground; there is no part way. Your family can't be afraid for their lives."

"I don't begin to know how to do that."

"I'd like to make a suggestion. Take care of your father first. One way or another, put him behind you. Then, when he no longer haunts you, let's talk about what to do with Sara. I'd bet it will be easier, like a heavy anvil has been lifted from around your neck."

"Thank you, that's helpful."

"I'll be with you in spirit when you confront your father."

"I'm glad…"

"Please remember this—you're nothing like him, nothing at all. You're a wise man, who's demonstrated to me your perceptiveness, your fine intelligence, and your good judgment. Rely on those qualities."

"I'll try… I'll have an advantage against him, since he won't know that I've freed the hostages, nor that his kidnappers were captured or killed."

"Yes, but please bear with me when I caution you, yet again. Never forget that you're dealing with someone who is capable of doing monstrous things that you could never imagine. So be prepared for that. Trust yourself, but get good help, and be ready to do whatever you have to do."

"You're a fine therapist, and a true friend. I'll call you when it's over."

◆◆◆

Back at the restaurant, Cash called the Macher. "Did you get the boat?"

"Yes, exactly as specified."

"When will it be ready and where?"

"Eleven, at one of the piers right on Elliott Bay. I'll meet him near the boat to give him the key."

"I'll want to be there too, out of sight."

"We can arrange that."

"I think I'd like Andre to be there as backup."

"I anticipated that. It's five after ten now. He's coming now to meet us at a coffee shop, Café Opla, on Alaskan Way, to be part of this conversation."

"Good, I'll meet you there… So you know, Samter sent the "all is well" wire as scheduled at ten. I saw it before he sent it."

"Perfect."

◆◆◆

Ten minutes later, Cash, Andre, and the Macher were getting coffee at a corner table.

"He's due to pick up the boat at eleven. He'll pick up the key from me. I'm meeting him in an office building on Elliott and Bell, just a few steps away, close to the dock. My friend rents a small office there, so it will be empty. The boat is moored near there. It's a big boat, forty-three feet. It sleeps four below. Your father will likely get there earlier to check it out… What are you thinking, Cash?" the Macher asked.

"Is there a place to hide in the office?"

"Yes, it has a bathroom."

"I'd like to hide in the bathroom, then when he comes in for the key, surprise him with a gun, read him the riot act, slap him senseless, handcuff him, then have Samter arrest him."

"Have you ever successfully surprised him?" Andre asked, unconvinced, plainly concerned.

"I've never tried."

"Well, I'd like to be there in case your civilized, courteous plan comes undone." Andre shook his head.

"You can hide down the hall to the office; there's a stairwell there," the Macher suggested. "I'll be there, too, in the office, giving him the key."

"He's relying on having the hostages, so this should be doable. He won't be expecting anything."

"Still, he's wily, and you've been a step behind him at every turn, which is unlike you." Andre looked up, pensive, then, when he worked it out, he offered, "I have to go shrinko. I'd say you keep screwing up since he's your father."

Cash smiled. "Dear God…be still my heart… Freud is back as a prosthetic-legged, Afro-Caribbean military strategist with a buzz cut…"

"Is that a dumbass white guy joke?"

"Maybe…let's start again, you are, after all, my good friend."

"And that's the only reason why I'll be there," Andre reiterated.

"Okay, you two," the Macher admonished. "Let's go check out the boat."

♦♦♦

At 10:25, the Macher was pointing out the spacious yacht. When that was done, they went to the nearby office building. Andre hid inside the stairwell, then the Macher let Cash into the empty office. It was old, but well-kept. There was a desk, a sitting area, a storage room, and a bathroom. Cash checked out both side rooms. He decided he'd hide in the storage room when the time came.

At 10:45, the Macher saw Kit from a window, checking out the boat. He nodded and sent Cash into the storage room.

At 10:55, the Macher opened the door to let Kit, Cash's father, into the office.

Kit wore a new, less noticeable patch on his left ear. "I looked over the boat outside. It looks adequate. I'll want you to unlock it and walk me through the entire boat until I'm satisfied."

"I'll do that, reluctantly."

"You'll do that with reverence, you sullied Jew filth…" Kit spit a wob of phlegm on the Macher's shirt.

The Macher cleaned the phlegm off his shirt with a handkerchief. "You're disgusting…"

"Watch your mouth, before I make you eat the next batch of snot and mucus…" He spit another wad of phlegm on the Macher's face. "Has the money been wired?"

The Macher used his handkerchief again, biting his tongue, hoping that Cash would appear soon. "Yes, you'll have it by one."

"All of it."

"Every dime you demanded, $8,000,000."

"Good, Jew boy, at least you can follow orders."

"If you insult me again, I'll withhold the boat."

"Unlikely, unless you want a fancy new necklace with little baby fingers, ears, and toes."

"You sick asshole," Cash snapped, as he stepped in, his gun drawn, pointed at his father's chest. "It's over. You foul-mouthed, vile piece of trash."

Kit took out his phone, held it up. "This is set for speed dial. All I need to do is press a number and your girlfriend and your grandson will die."

Cash stepped in front of him, set his gun down on the desk, then grabbed his father's left shoulder with his left hand and slapped him forcefully with his right hand across the face. When Kit fell back, Cash pulled him forward again with his left hand, then slapped him again with his right, stronger still, across his father's face. "Press the button, you vicious bastard. Callie and the baby are home safely. Your men are in prison or dead." Cash slapped him again, even harder. "This is long overdue," he announced, loudly, as Kit fell.

Kit fell back, crying out, his backside landing against the desk.

"Your life of bullying, humiliating, and intimidating people is over." Cash declared. "Get ready to die in prison."

"You're lying. What you said is impossible."

"Try it. Gus is dead."

"If that's true, you'll pay for it dearly, in new, excruciating ways."

"It's your turn to pay." Cash grabbed his throat. "I'm thinking about how you killed my mother, captured and vulgarly tortured me, set a bomb that injured my daughter, then captured my girlfriend and my grandson. I'm weighing right now whether to kill you."

Kit pressed another button on his phone. "We'll see about that, you worthless rat boy."

Without warning, the door flew open, and two men, disguised as dock workers, entered expertly, knees dropping to the floor, putting semi-automatic weapons on Cash and the Macher. They were clearly experienced and well-trained.

Cash's weapon was useless, lying on the desk. One of the men covered them, while the other closed the door, then returned to pointing his semi-automatic pistol at first Cash, then the Macher.

Kit stood, then let out a blood-curdling yell. "Who's going to die now, you pansy ass rat turd." He picked up Cash's gun and crashed it across his face.

Cash yelled when his father smashed his face, yet again. "Did you ever think you could stop me? As a boy, I know you thought, worried, that I'd kill your hopeless mother. Did you also know she was good for nothing except sex, and I had to teach her how to please me. By the end, she was like a well-trained whore." He raised the gun, cracked Cash's face again. "I should have killed you then. Made your mother watch me torture you, before I slit your throat." He cracked the gun against the top of his head, harder still. Cash went down on his knees. Kit held forth, savoring this, "Rat turd, you know what happened to Chen, the traitor? I tricked him this morning, then one of my men cut off his tiny penis and made him swallow it." Kit laughed. "I watched this, on a Zoom. I talked to him. He wants to give me my ear back, today…" Kit laughed, loudly, then explained, "You're going to get far worse. You'll taste agonizing, heartbreaking, shame right here, before you die." Kit laughed again as he carefully pointed the gun at Cash's crotch.

Cash saw Andre slowly open the door, inch by inch. He yelled at Kit, a distraction, "Fuck you, old man, you're worse than a crazed, rabid dog."

Cash dropped, lying on the floor, as Andre fired two shots through the open door, instantly bringing down Kit and one of the thugs. During the exchange, Andre took a bullet in his good leg. The Macher shot the second thug twice, killing him. He'd drawn his own gun from a holster on his hip when Kit pressed the button on his phone, then hid the gun under his jacket. As he went down, though, the second thug put a bullet in the Macher's left shoulder.

Cash looked around, looking to his father on the floor. His father was wounded, but he had Cash's gun trained on Cash.

Kit cried out, "Know my vengeance…." then louder still, "You pansy ass rat turd," he screamed, poised to fire. At just the same time, the Macher and Andre each shot him—one in the arm and one in the hand holding the gun. Kit let the gun drop.

Cash stood over him. "You sick, vile bastard. I'm not going to kill you today…I'm having you arrested, but you're going to spend the rest of your life in prison."

Andre and the Macher, though wounded, helped Cash stand up, set him down on the desk. The Macher kept his gun on Kit as Andre limped into the bathroom, tied a towel around the wound on his bleeding leg, then tossed a towel over to the Macher. Andre put his gun on Kit, then turned to Cash from the bathroom door. "You keep making the same damn mistake," he said. "This asshole may have been your father, but even from prison, he'll find a way to hurt you and your loved ones again."

"What are you saying?" Cash asked.

The Macher and Andre looked at each other, nodded, then each of them shot Kit in the head.

◆◆◆

Cash called Samter right away, who arrived in ten minutes. Cash had told him that he was hoping to bring in his father and asked him to be standing by. As soon as Samter came in, he distributed first aid kits, which Cash had requested, to Andre and the Macher. He looked at both of them, then said, "I'll call an ambulance. You need to be treated at the hospital. In the meantime, these will fix you up better than a washcloth."

Samter looked at the wounded men, who were dressing their injuries, then the three dead men. "Didn't go as you planned."

"He surprised us with two extra men," Cash explained. "Fortunately, Andre was backing us up."

Samter looked closely at Kit. "Did you have to shoot him twice in the head?"

Andre looked up from his leg and nodded, "Hell, yes. Can't be too careful with a guy like this."

"God knows he deserved it."

The Macher adjusted a bandage, then turned to Samter, "Ed, so you know, Cash hoped to arrest him. We didn't even give him a chance. It was just too damned dangerous. His father was grabbing Cash's gun off the floor. So it was self-defense."

"Don't even try to explain that to me. I'm just glad you are all alive, and that this monster is dead..." Samter looked at the other dead men.

Andre tried to stand on his wounded leg. He couldn't. He sat back down on the desk.

Samter turned back. He paused, then smiled at his three friends. "Indulge me. I have to say this. I finally have a way of thinking about you guys—being friends with you, working with you, it's like being in a Tarantino movie."

"What?" Andre asked, confused. "Who?"

"Quentin Tarantino, the filmmaker. I was thinking about *Pulp Fiction*."

"What the hell are you talking about?"

"It's a movie, Andre." The Macher stepped right up, "…and yes, he's right. Andre is Travolta as Vince Vega. He's perfect, even the dancing. And Cash is Samuel Jackson as Jules. And remember this when you go to talk with your daughter later, Jules retires from his life of crime to live a more peaceful existence."

Cash shook his head.

Samter went on, "It works, doesn't it. It just came to me rewatching the movie with my girlfriend several days ago. Like you guys, nothing is like it's supposed to be—crazy, violent things happen out of nowhere, and important things often work out against all odds in unexpected ways."

Cash laughed out loud. "This is unprecedented, Detective Samter as a profound philosopher of complex, contemporary cinema. It's as likely as Andre being another Freud."

"I give up," Andre said. "Don't even start that shit."

Cash smiled. "Okay, I've got to call Callie."

◆◆◆

Cash stepped outside. Callie picked up right away.

"It's over, babe. Really over."

"Is that bastard dead? Really dead? None of this bullshit like life in prison?"

"Yes, in spite of my efforts to put him in prison."

"Did your friends do that?"

"Yes, without my approval."

"You have wonderful, smart friends. I'm so relieved that they took charge. You can't imagine. Every now and then, your well-hidden moral scruples need to be soundly overruled. Especially when it relates to your father."

"You're right. I have to say it."

"Thank you. Now let me guess, you want to see Abe before you come home?"

"How did I ever get such a smart, even prescient, woman?"

"She's very lucky. Before you get off, your smart, prescient woman wants to tell you that she went to bat for you with your daughter."

"Was it hard?"

"She is really pissed, but she agreed to give you twenty-four hours. I had to play every favor she owed me. You better go to work, the clock is ticking."

"Thank you. I'm getting Abe on it."

"Tell him you need the miracle of Hanukkah, minimum."

"What?"

"He'll understand."

"Will you please tell Sara that my father, her grandfather, is dead and that I didn't kill him? Tell her how it happened. Also, please ask her if we can talk this evening. I should have something to begin a conversation by then."

"Sweetheart, '*begin a conversation*' won't cut it."

"Then tell her whatever you think will work. I'll try to have something to keep her from leaving by then."

"I hope your therapist is really, really damn good."

"We'll see…" Cash paused, then asked, "Babe, am I like Samuel Jackson in *Pulp Fiction*?"

"What, are you crazy? You're way cooler than Samuel Jackson."

◆◆◆

Cash called Abe, worked out a time to see him, then went back inside. "I have to go," he explained. "Do you need my help with anything here before I leave?"

Samter responded, "There's an ambulance on the way to take your friends to the hospital, and there are my men coming to bring these bodies to the morgue. You'll have to do some paperwork and identify your father's body, but you can take care of that later."

"Thank you. I have to see Abe now. After, I'll come check on both of you at the hospital."

Andre, who was sitting on the desk asked, "How many times a day do you see your therapist?"

"Andre, do you like being annoying?"

"You make it so easy. And, incidentally, I liked you more when you didn't think so much about yourself."

"You never think about yourself, and I still like you." He turned to the Macher, "Are you okay?"

"Yeah, I'm fine. We'll catch up later."

"Thank you and Andre. I needed both of you."

"That was obvious," Andre muttered.

Cash ignored him. "Ed, thank you, too."

"Backing you guys up is my most unpredictable, favorite part of policework."

◆◆◆

Twenty minutes later, Cash was in his red chair in Abe's office. "It's over," he explained. "I tried to have him arrested, but the Macher and Andre took matters into their own hands. They each shot him in the head."

"Just like that?"

"Before I could say a word to stop them."

"Are you okay with it?"

"I'd decided I wouldn't kill him, that I'd send him to prison, but they took it out of my hands… After they killed him, I was relieved that they did it."

"I understand that. Your friends, who obviously care deeply about you, must have seen that it had to be done. They also knew that you wouldn't do it. So they took charge. They took care of their close friend. It's not what I would have guessed, but it's an acceptable outcome, even a relief."

"They were right about him. He was truly horrific—at his very worst at the end. Still, I thought you didn't want me to kill him."

"I didn't want *you* to kill him, he's *your* father."

"Is it easier to live with it if my friends killed my father?"

"We'll find out, but I'll bet that it is. And what I like about this is that you didn't ask them to, tell them to, or even know that they were going to do it."

"I don't think I'll ever be okay with it."

"No, he'll always be your father, but you can learn to live with it, not be preoccupied with it, or overly troubled by it."

"I'm not there yet."

"There's time. Can I change the subject for a moment?"

"Of course."

"The headaches, the angry outbursts, you're doing better with those, aren't you?"

"How did you know?"

"Even with the danger, the violence, the chaos, you've been more focused, less distracted."

"That's possible… Yes, I think so."

"Most people who have the kind of symptoms you presented become more anxious, more withdrawn, far more preoccupied in the face of real frightening danger. You were facing a maniacal, murderous father attacking you and your family. During that, you were clear-headed, calm, and capable."

"Thank you. I think that when the danger became real, when it wasn't just a dream, or a childhood fantasy, or a confusing memory, when the very worst really happened, my own father trying to kill me and my loved ones, it was somehow possible for me to confront it.

I knew I had to stop this frightening person, and I knew that the man I am today could do that."

"Yes, and that must be good to know."

"It is...does that mean that this problem is over?"

"Not quite yet, but for now, just know that you've weathered the storm, admirably, and just knowing that will help you if the headaches, the angry incidents, the depression, reappear."

"I hope so. But before I can even begin to feel better, I have to figure out how to work things out with my daughter."

"Have you even had time to think about that?"

"Not really. She wants me to change my entire way of life, everything. Essentially—and truthfully, I understand her—she doesn't want what I do to ever put her family at risk. I have no idea how to think about it, and even less about how to change it."

"Is it important enough to you that you'd try to make that kind of change?"

"Yes, absolutely."

"It may mean giving up things that you're used to, that you care about."

"I'm sure it will, and I'm prepared to do that if, at the end of the day, it can work for all of us. Although she hasn't said it, I'm sure Sara realizes that this can't possibly work out if it doesn't work for both of us. In fact, that's part of the problem. I think she's convinced that it's impossible for us because she doesn't see a way that I will be happy with it."

"What does Callie say about it?"

"Though she wouldn't say it, I think she'd like it too... But it will be a problem for her if she has to give up her restaurant. We haven't even begun to talk about that..."

"Could she live with taking time away, letting others run it for some period?"

"Maybe...we'd have to talk about how that might work, and for how long. There's an immediate problem, though. Sara has given me twenty-four hours to come up with a solution. That's sometime tomorrow, and

I don't begin to know what that kind of change even looks like, for either Callie or me."

Abe looked away toward the far wall, pensive. After a long minute, he turned back. "I'm going to suggest something that's unconventional, but time is of the essence, and I have an idea… Is your partner available?"

"I'm sure she'd work it out to be available for this."

"I'd like her to join our conversation, right away. This is a conversation that she should be part of… It's one thirty. I'm available between three and four. Let's reconvene, the three of us, here at three. Okay?"

"Done."

CHAPTER EIGHT

Cash called Callie to set up the 3:00 appointment with Abe, then stopped by the hospital. At the hospital, he saw that the Macher and Andre had somehow managed to be put in the same room, and now, each of them was being prepared by a nurse to have their bullets removed and then their wounds properly cleaned, treated, and bandaged. Cash managed to confirm that they were both alright—the nurses reassured him that their respective procedures were not life-threatening, and that they could be released by tomorrow or the day after. Andre was showing his nurse the tattoo of two naked Vietnamese women on his chest. He was showing the nurse how he could make the girls dance—some people said make love—by flexing his muscles. She was smiling, and Cash was already willing to bet that she'd be having dinner with Andre tomorrow or the night after. He waved at Andre, who, busy with the nurse, ignored him, then he pulled a chair next to the Macher.

"How are you feeling?" Cash asked.

"I'm fine, eager to get out of here. I don't do well in hospitals."

"I'll figure out how to get you out this evening after they take out the bullet and patch you up."

"Thanks. How are you?"

"I'm glad it's over, though I didn't expect my father to die. I'm still thinking about that, conflicted about it."

"We didn't plan on killing your father. But truthfully, it was simply the obvious thing, the only thing, to do, as soon as you started talking about prison. He was absolutely, dangerously out of control, easily the most disgusting human being I've ever known. If there wasn't irrefutable proof, I'd never believe he was really your father."

"So you never had any hesitation about killing him?"

"None. Not ever… Hell, if we hadn't done that, I promise you he'd have found a way to have you, Callie, Lew, Sara, and Young Cash, all of you, killed from prison in maybe his first month in."

"I should have known that when he spit on you, and called you a kike, he was a dead man."

"No kidding. Were you ready to forgive him for urinating on you, several times? Telling you—what did he say—how you had to taste the shame?"

"No, that was really awful. Worst of all for me is how he took my grandson, my partner, and absolutely terrified my daughter."

"I understand. Where do things stand with Sara?"

"She's given me an ultimatum. I have to completely change my way of life, change myself. I can't ever put any of us in danger again. Anything less, she won't allow me in her, or in her family's, life. She's adamant. I don't know what to do."

"Cash, you're a fine, wonderful man, as dear a friend as I've ever had. I have only one thing to say to you—work this out with Sara, whatever you have to do, whatever it takes. Just make it work."

◆◆◆

After leaving Harborview, Cash took a walk. He wasn't going anywhere. All he knew was that he needed some time alone, time to process all that had happened before he'd be able to keep his new, now very fragile family together. He knew he had reason to feel good, good that the perilous demon who'd been stalking his family and friends was dead. But he didn't feel good. Rather, he was overwhelmed, sinking in the swamp, unable to think clearly about how to respond to his daughter.

He'd known her almost two years, and during that time, she'd captivated him, touched his heart, and when her son, his grandson, was born, it was certainly one of the happiest days of his life. Everything had changed for him, gotten immeasurably better, since the day she arrived. He remembered all of it, every moment. How they'd worked together to get her identity back, how they brought her murderous identity thieves to unexpected rough justice. He'd never forget how she'd saved his life, more than once. How she'd married a fine Cuban man, Alvaro, had a child, and now, all of that—all of it—was at risk. If he couldn't have Sara and her family in his life, he knew it would be unbearable.

He found a bench to sit down where he could look out over the water. What could he possibly do that would convince her that he'd changed, really changed, that he'd work it out so that they could live safely? He'd considered new work, but he couldn't imagine going to an office every day, nor did he have any idea what kind of business would hire him. Most importantly, a new job wouldn't satisfy Sara. He thought about moving—New York, Miami, even Paris—but it wouldn't necessarily change his life, his work, and if not, it wouldn't be enough for Sara. Also, he couldn't ask Callie to give up her restaurant forever. Besides, he liked what he did, where he lived, especially liked his eccentric ragtag group of friends, and madly loved the woman he lived with. He checked his watch. Time to get to Abe's office, he didn't want to be late. Callie had said she'd meet him there. He stood up, walked back toward the hospital where he'd left his car. He didn't know what to do, he didn't even know how to think about it. At times like this, when he was stuck, he'd learned to listen to people he respected, then rely on his instincts. He already knew that the Macher was right. He had to make this work. Okay then, let Abe take the next step. Cash realized he was glad Callie would be there.

◆◆◆

At 3:02, Cash and Callie were sitting around a circular wooden table that Abe kept in his office across the room from his desk. Abe had seated them in comfortable wooden chairs with leather seats, and he'd just started talking, "First, thank you, Callie, for coming on such short notice."

"This is important, I'd like to help if I can."

"I suspect you can," Abe offered. "Cash, would you like to take the lead?"

Cash frowned, "As you know, I'm confounded as to what I could, should, do. I think if you got us started, it might help me."

"Okay. I'm not prepared to offer any suggestions yet, but I'd like to ask some questions. First, how willing is Sara to compromise? Is there a way to meet in the middle, like spend several months a year together?"

Callie responded, "No, is the short answer. Sara will not compromise. She will not spend any time at all with her dad, so long as it's even remotely possible that anything he's involved in could attract danger of any kind. She's absolutely unyielding about that."

"Is that as broad as it sounds?" Abe asked.

"Even broader," Callie explained. "She'd lose her father rather than ever put her family in this kind of danger again. She's very smart. She knows that they could be in a car accident in Miami or Cuba or caught in an earthquake in South America somewhere or be exposed to any number of terrible diseases. But she believes that Cash, and his way of life, brings unacceptable risks that can, and need to be eliminated."

Cash nodded, then added, "As she put it, 'there's an unstoppable curse in our family where innocent people keep dying…' I don't want Baby Cash to grow up in this frightening, dangerous world we're somehow caught in."

"Is it possible that she'll ever become more flexible, more willing to compromise as she gets beyond this?"

"No, I know Sara," Cash nodded. "I also remember one other unforgettable thing she said, and I quote, 'What we're on right now, is a very fast train, an unstoppable, runaway train that will kill more of our family and close friends.' Again and again. Next time, it could be Lew or Alvaro, it could be the Macher or Andre."

Abe nodded. "She's smart and articulate like her father. I'm understanding the problem. Anything else she's said that might give us some direction?"

"I'll paraphrase the rest of that statement. She explained, 'I'm about to get off of this train. We have to go far away from you…Miami, even Cuba…to have a chance to be able to really, truly get off… But there's no middle ground. Unless you can somehow get off—genuinely get off, forever—we'll never have a chance.'"

Abe took a beat, looking at the ceiling, thinking, then turned back, "All right…I have one possible idea…it's not a final solution, but it's a way to start, to stay together while you work this out…can I try it out on you?"

"Yes, please," Cash replied.

"Suppose all of you—that's primarily Sara, Alvaro, Baby Cash, Cash, and Callie—take time off, a year would be good, living together, traveling on a boat. You can work out your itinerary together. Callie, you'd have to take time off from your restaurant, but you could keep it open and fly in periodically to check on it. Other people, like Lew, could join when they can. All of you, Callie and Cash, Sara and Alvaro, would have to agree that you'd stay with it to work over this year to come to a long-term solution."

Callie smiled. "Okay, yes… I love this idea."

Cash was less convinced. "Why? You'd have to share a bathroom."

"Sara and I will set up his and her bathrooms. And that will be fine… Babe, it's not just a well-deserved break; it's a total change of life, an adventure, a chance to regroup, rethink how we want to live the rest of our lives."

Cash was thinking, warming up to the idea. "Sara would love it. She lived on a boat as a teenager with her mother…and it would be totally safe…it also gives us time to be together while we think about how to do something long term."

Abe nodded. "That's where the idea came from. It was a safe way for Corey and I to plan carefully, leisurely for the future. Corey lived on a boat a lot. She taught me about how being away for long periods frees you up, makes other things possible. Before we were married, when she was in danger, she took her son and her boat to hide up the Inside Passage. I found her, jumped out of a float plane to be with her—"

Callie interrupted, "Are you kidding? You, Abe Stein, jumped out of an airplane into the freezing cold water of the Inside Passage?"

"I did. I was younger, and I couldn't swim, so I put on an extra large lifejacket and jumped into the ocean right near her boat. It was freezing cold…I was shaking…she pulled me out of the water when she finally figured out who I was…I stayed with her on the boat for a long time. It's when I proposed to her, when we decided how we wanted to live, when we decided to take on Nick Season. Everything we ever did and became was started in the wilderness on that boat."

"I'd love to go by boat up the Inside Passage," Callie volunteered.

Abe nodded. "If you do that, you could leave in the spring. You could go all the way to Alaska in the summer and then back down to California by October or November."

"How can we convince Sara and her family to do this?" Cash asked.

"The person to talk to about this is my wife, Corey. She spent many years living on her boat with her mom. That's actually something that she has in common with Sara. Corey knows this whole coast like the back of her hand."

"I have an idea," Callie said. "This is outside standard procedure, but Abe, why don't you and Corey come for dinner with us tonight at our restaurant? I'll also invite Sara and her family. We only have a short time to come to an agreement, and I'm sure you and Corey could answer questions, talk about what it would be like, and generally help make this work. Cash, is this okay with you?"

"I think it's a good idea. Are you comfortable with it, Abe?"

"I'm comfortable with our working relationship, and knowing you, having dinner won't do any harm. Most importantly, anything I can do that will help you keep your new-found family intact is worth trying. I'll ask Corey."

"Let's meet early, say six thirty, so we have plenty of time. Will that be okay?"

"I think so."

"This is the first idea that has a chance of working," Cash said. "I need to think about what it would mean for me, and of course, Callie, you will too, but we can talk about all of that together tonight. Should I call Sara and explain our hopes for dinner, who's coming and so on?"

"If it's okay with you," Callie put her hand on Cash's forearm, "I think I should invite her and Alvaro, and without mentioning the idea, simply say we've been working on a plan to keep the family together. I will add that Abe has been helping us, and he thinks his wife, Corey, can be helpful going forward, so they've also been invited. I'm sure she'll want to hear us out, and it will be easier for her to keep an open mind if it comes from me."

"You're right," Cash covered her hand, and turned to Abe. "Thank you, Abe. It's just a beginning, but you've given me some hope. We'll see you tonight."

◆◆◆

In the car, Callie called Sara. Callie presented the thinking behind, and the plan for, dinner. Sara was skeptical but agreed to come with Alvaro and the baby. Before ending the conversation, she added, "I'm looking forward to spending some time with Abe and his wife. What kind of therapist goes to dinner with his patient?"

"The same kind that kills the man who's threatening to kill his wife-to-be. He's unconventional, he's smart, and he's very good at what he does. I can sincerely say that he wants to keep your family together."

"I like him for that, though honestly, I don't see a way to do that."

"Your dad, especially, has been working hard, and Abe had a good idea. Give it a chance."

"I'll listen, that's all I can say."

"Good. Thank you. See you at six thirty."

At the restaurant, Callie got Will and Jill to help her rearrange the tables downstairs, putting a round table in a private area that they created in the back corner. In that spot, the six of them could talk privately, and there was space for a crib beside them for the baby.

Cash had gone to the hospital to check on Itzac and Andre. He called Callie, who picked up from the dining room. "Hey babe, they're both fine."

"Good."

"A question: I was able to get the Macher released, and it occurred to me that he might be helpful at dinner. Sara adores him and respects him. He'll absolutely like this idea. I can fill him in on the way back."

"Good idea, he'll fit right in, though he doesn't strike me as a man of the sea."

"He'll be himself, and he'll help."

"Invite him. I'll add a seventh chair. Andre may not be such a good idea."

"Not to worry, he's very busy courting his nurse."

"Good all around. See you soon."

◆◆◆

At 6:40, all seven of them were drinking wine around the table, and the baby was sleeping in his crib beside the table. Cash began, "Sara, we've been working to find a way to keep our family together. I'm going to ask Abe to present where we are."

Abe stood, "To begin, let's toast this entire family, with special attention to Sara and Cash." All seven glasses touched, a heartfelt salute, then Abe went on, "It's been my privilege to get to know Cash and through him, to get to know more about all of you. As I've learned about your situation, I've seen that Sara's concerns and issues are real, and Cash's desire to respond helpfully to those concerns is also real. So, I'm going to begin at the end, with what we'd like to suggest—it's an initial, interim step, but it's a good start. Put simply, I propose that the five of you spend a year living together on a comfortable boat, traveling on an itinerary as yet to be worked out, working together to solve this problem."

Sara was curious. "All of us on a boat for a year?"

"Yes," Abe replied. "I'm going to turn this over to Corey, who took me on her boat to live together when she was in danger. It's when I proposed marriage, and we figured out the next steps in the rest of our lives…Corey?"

Corey began, "Sara, I understand you lived on a boat in the Mediterranean with your mother."

"I did, for five years until I turned nineteen."

"So you'll understand this. I, too, grew up on a boat with my mom. I kept that boat for many years after my mother died, then replaced it, after it was destroyed. It's still a refuge for me when I need to get away to figure out confusing things. One of the things I've learned is that when you're moving from place to place on a boat, no one knows who, or where, you are unless you want them to. No one will bother you, and you have the time, the rhythm, the uninterrupted space to think long and hard about whatever you need or want to… Or, if you want to lie in the sun and do absolutely nothing, you can just do that, for as long as you'd like. Put another way, you're free, in charge of yourself. Excepting weather, there's nothing else outside in the world to force your decisions."

"I remember that, and I remember long hours when my mother would tell me stories or myths or just memories. These were the happiest times in my childhood," Sara said.

"My mother told me all the Greek myths, the tragedies, about fate and Moira, and my favorite, all about the gods—Zeus, Poseidon, Apollo, Aphrodite, Athena, and more. Those are still wonderful memories," Corey confirmed, smiling.

Sara frowned. "What will it be like on a boat with four adults and a baby?"

"You'll figure it out, find a rhythm, a pattern, and don't forget, you can stop on land, at a sandy shore, or on a remote island, and spend as long as you'd like. Anytime. You can camp out, sleep on the beach, make a fire, and cook the fish you've caught. We have a cabin up the Inside Passage, and if you choose to go that way, you can stay there as long as you'd like. If you do decide to go up the Inside Passage, I'll sit down and go over a map with those of you who'd like that. I'll mark uninhabited islands, pristine sandy beaches, wonderful fishing, clamming and crab spots, places to see whales, nesting bald eagles, and so on, and areas to be careful of the bears. I have a lifetime of traveling, of living, up there, and I'd happily share it with you."

The Macher, who'd been listening, jumped in, "It sounds so good that I may invite myself for at least a month."

Callie said, "I, for one, would love it if you came." Others, including Sara, nodded in agreement.

Sara turned to her father. "Dad, would you actually commit to staying with the boat for a year? No side trips, no planes back to some remote place to close some deal, or back to Seattle to meet with a trading partner."

"Yes, I will promise you that."

"No exceptions, period."

"Yes, I will stay with the boat for a year. No exceptions, period."

"That helps."

Callie turned to Corey, "If Sara agrees to this plan, Corey, would you talk to us about where we might go? I've been fantasizing about the Inside Passage, Alaska, California, even Mexico. I'd also be interested in Europe or the Caribbean and South America."

"Any of those are possible. Take your time. If you want to go to Europe or South America, you'll want to rent a boat there. Choosing the boat you want is an important decision, and that will take some homework. For such a big trip with at least four adults and a baby, you need a good, comfortable boat. That won't be cheap."

The Macher stepped up, again. "I'm a committed believer in keeping this family together. I'm also absolutely in favor of this plan to make it happen. I'd like to make a contribution to help. As such, I'll rent whatever boat you choose. Don't worry about the cost. Pick a boat that you'll love even more after a year."

"That's too much, too generous," Cash said.

"It's worth every penny if this works out. I can't even put a price on the cost of putting up with you if your family falls apart."

Callie went over and hugged the Macher. "Thank you, Itzac, you're a remarkable friend." She turned to Sara, "Sara, if you'll agree to do this, I'll promise that you and I will set up his and her separate bathrooms."

Sara stood. "I've listened carefully, and I, too, would like to keep this family together. And yes, I believe that this is an idea that we should try. Especially since you're all being so helpful to make it work. Itzac, I count you in my family, and you take my breath away. Callie, you answered my last question. Dad, I realize what a change you're making for me. How complicated, how difficult much of it will be for you. I didn't think it was possible to love you anymore, but I do." She turned into her father's warm embrace.

Still teary, Sara stepped back and then, to everyone, "This won't be easy, but I'll do my best."

EPILOGUE

(ONE YEAR LATER, SIX MONTHS AT SEA)

Their boat, a fifty-two-foot Chris-Craft, was anchored in a remote bay, tucked away at the tip of a pear-shaped island near the Fiordland Provincial Recreation Area, a 225,000-acre mountainous wilderness of islands, inlets, fiords, waterfalls, rivers, and glaciers. It was a beautiful, wild, hard-to-reach stretch of the Inside Passage, and it was a welcome interlude, a lovely way for the five of them to be together safely.

They'd taken almost six months to get ready to leave. Cash and Callie had carefully organized their lives to be away for a year. Callie had left Will in charge of the restaurant and agreed to come back every four months. They'd stay in touch via email and cell phone as needed. Cash had simply shut down his business—finishing all of his pending deals, walking away from his new unfinished deal with the Macher, refusing to take on any other new business. Cash continued to meet regularly with Abe, working together until they both felt he was able to move on comfortably.

During the time before leaving, they'd searched regularly to find the proper boat. Alvaro, Andre, and the Macher all worked together to help them find it. Sara and her family had gone back to Cuba to feel safe, at ease, during the months before leaving. Alvaro came back to Seattle as needed to help choose the boat. Early on, Sara and Alvaro, along with Cash and Callie, had spent a long time with Corey before deciding they'd go up the Inside Passage. They never regretted that decision.

Now, it was a year after they decided to try this, and they'd spent a little more than six months of that time on the boat. Over that time, they'd learned to travel well as a family. They'd grown even closer on the boat and though they hadn't found an answer, they'd had many positive and helpful conversations about their future together. Significantly, over time, all of them had grown fully committed to finding a long-term way to live their lives together.

For the past three days, they'd been staying at an old hunting and fishing cabin that Abe and Corey had stayed in when they first got together, then bought and fixed it up. The cabin sat on a bluff several hundred yards north of an unexpected sandy beach. At the end of the long, wind-swept beach, there was a creek where salmon came to spawn. From the beach, you could look through the little bay across a wide inlet to a sheer cliff climbing straight into the sky.

Today, on the beach, they'd gathered wood and set up a fire for cooking. Cash and Callie had set a grill over the fire on four big stones. Now, they tended to the fire, sitting on logs they'd set around the grill. Cash watched Baby Cash, now sixteen months old, busy playing with a toy truck on a blanket beside him. The baby liked to wander out on the beach to fill his truck with sand. Cash would gently bring him back. In the distance, they could see Sara and Alvaro walking back from the creek.

At the mouth of the creek, they'd been catching salmon, using herring they'd been catching with a herring rake as bait. Alvaro, a seasoned fisherman, had fashioned the rake with a twelve-foot cedar stick with the lower portion studded with about thirty inches of sharp, pointed nails. Yesterday morning, Sara, who'd learned to love fishing when she'd lived on the boat with her mom, and Alvaro had successfully raked for herring in the bay from their dinghy. That afternoon, they'd caught salmon for dinner. This evening was no exception. They arrived at the fire to show Cash and Callie four fine silver salmon. Near the grill, they'd already set up a wooden plank where Alvaro would clean the fresh fish. He left the fish in an ice-filled cooler there, since it was still early for dinner, especially since this far north, in the summer, it was light well after 10:00 a.m. At the moment, it was only 5:00 p.m., and the sun was shining brightly. Cash passed the baby, who'd started crying, over to Sara, who knew what he wanted. She sat him on her lap, then gently presented a bottle, which Baby Cash eagerly took as he began feeding. When he wandered over to the blanket, Alvaro took over, and walked him down the beach. Before long, Cash expertly served Bombay Blue Sapphire martinis with extra olives to each of them. He'd perfected his signature version of this cocktail on their trip. He raised his glass to present a toast.

At that moment, they saw two helicopters in the distance. They were mid-sized helicopters, each of them capable of carrying four or five people comfortably.

"What?" Alvaro asked. "Are we in trouble?"

"I have no idea," Cash said, then set down his martini, eyeing the helicopters.

Alvaro stood. "I'll check it out."

Callie took his arm and shook her head, no.

"What? What is this? Who are these people?" Cash called out. "We're in the middle of the wilderness."

Callie took Cash's hand, smiling, "What day is tomorrow?"

"Saturday?"

"Yes…Saturday, August seventeenth. Happy Birthday!" she said.

"Oh my God." He smiled at her. "I lost track of the dates way out here."

"Fiftieth is a big event, and I don't think you'll be disappointed."

"How did you organize this?"

"Sara helped. Between us, it was easy."

Cash took Sara's hand, squeezing gently, then held Callie's hand tenderly with his other hand.

The helicopters landed on the beach nearby, then turned off their engines. When the blades stopped revolving, someone inside, in the closest one, turned on a boom box at full volume. "Happy Birthday" came thundering down the beach as people started coming down out of the helicopter singing to the music. In no time, Andre, the Macher, Lew, Abe and Corey, Samter and Katie, Lincoln and Cherry all made their way toward the fire on the beach, singing yet another raucous verse of "Happy Birthday." They carried a colorful cloth banner, "Happy 50th birthday, Cash!" signed by all of them, including pictures and colorful drawings.

In no time at all, the fire was expanded, more driftwood logs were brought around to sit on. Samter, Lincoln, and Andre unloaded supplies—trays, boxes, even full coolers, from the helicopter. Apparently, under Callie's supervision, Césaire had created a special birthday dinner. Appetizers were spread out—cheeses, foie gras with pear sauce, pate crostini with blackberry jam, baked feta bites, garlicky shrimp cocktails, melon prosciutto skewers, bite-sized crab cakes with mango-avocado relish, a variety of breads, and much more. Beer, wine, a variety of alcohols, and mixers were set out. Andre took charge of pouring drinks and offering exotic cocktails.

When everyone was comfortably settled in, the Macher stood. "This is a very special, wonderful occasion. My dearest friend is turning fifty, and we're all here to make it an unforgettable event. Most importantly, we're joining him as he's making a major transition in his life, as he's considering substantial, hard-to-imagine changes. What I propose is that all of us share things we know about Cash, things that make him remarkable, things that won't change, that will stay with him, whatever he becomes. Also, please feel free to share things about making changes in your own lives that may be useful in thinking about this. There are no rules, it is simply a way of participating in the conversation he is surely having, with the hope of helping him think about this transition."

Cash smiled, "That would be great. I can use all of the help I can get."

The Macher nodded. "Good...let's slow down and take our time creating a memorable festive occasion. Enjoy the appetizers, the drinks, then, when we're done toasting, and talking about Cash, we'll feast. Callie and Césaire have prepared a fantastic dinner—featuring cassoulet with duck confit, game sausages (wild boar, elk, and venison), roast suckling pig, lamb stew, truffle risotto, roasted squash salad, potage lyonnais, and more. We have at least five hours before dark. We have plenty of space in the house, and we'll pitch some tents on the bluff so everyone will have somewhere comfortable to sleep...so now, let's celebrate our dear friend Cash. If I may begin?"

Glasses were raised, touched, a "yes" to the Macher.

He turned toward Cash, "I remember almost three years ago. Cash and Callie had brought Sara to my apartment in old West Greenwich Village, in New York City. Cash and Sara were on their way to sneak into Cuba to begin some very dangerous business. I'd never met Sara, and I was instantly struck by how much she was like Cash—in manner, in her appearance, her sharp intelligence, and her quiet, understated style—how wonderful they were together, and, of course, Sara captivated me, won me over immediately. Though no one could explain exactly how it happened, I was playing the piano, accompanying Sara, and then Cash, who were improvising a rendition of a song, actually singing Willie Nelson's version of "Crazy," together for the very first time. Sara and Cash had somehow worked it out, and they sang remarkably well together. It was as if they'd done this before. I was dumbfounded, astonished by how naturally these two people communicated so easily without even talking. It was a brief respite, a moment of joyfulness, genuine sweetness, amidst the deadly gamble they'd entered into. In truth, it was a celebration, a little moment of father and daughter finding something in common that they'd come to love separately, then making a connection, unexpectedly, when finding each other after so many long years. Until then, I didn't even know that Cash was a fine singer, and that's why I tell this story, Cash is a very modest man of so many talents. But what I'll always remember is how he revealed that strength in this brilliantly rendered expression of love for his newfound daughter. My point is that whatever this man chooses to become, he'll always surprise us with his sensitivity, his intelligence, his depth, and his generous heart. It really doesn't matter what he decides, so long as it works for his daughter, and, of course, his girlfriend, Callie. Whatever he decides, I know he'll find his own way to be true to himself."

Everyone raised their glasses, crying out, "Bravo!"

Then, at that moment, Sara brought her baby back to play with Alvaro in the sand near the group. She came behind her father, put her hands on his shoulder, and began singing "Crazy." Cash joined in effortlessly, and everyone was spellbound as they sang so beautifully together.

When the cheering died down, Sara offered another song, "Tonight is What It Means To Be Young," from the movie *Streets of Fire*. She explained that when they first met, she and Alvaro started playing a game of testing each other about old movies, a game they still played and enjoyed. *Streets of Fire* was the first one, and the one that brought them together. She pointed at Alvaro, who pointed back, then she dedicated this splendid, poignant song to her dad. It was a lovely rendition. By the second verse, her dad was singing with her.

When the applause died down, Samter stood, raised his glass. "I first met Callie soon after her ex-husband was hit by a car and blown threw her restaurant's front glass window. I met Cash later, well after Callie's restaurant was set on fire, and one of Cash's best friends was killed. He was always evasive, in the background. She did most of the talking, and she was evasive, too. Callie cut me out, systematically, of all of the things I needed to know. I later understood that Cash was behind her refusal to share information with me. Later still, Cash was kidnapped, and once again, they kept me out of it.

I was fed up, ready to arrest both of them, when, unexpectedly, they delivered Avi and Christy Ben-Meyer, vicious criminals—murderers, identity thieves, and money launderers—to me. Unbelievably, they next delivered Amjad Hasim, thought dead—a terrorist, arms dealer, and worse—who they miraculously discovered in San Diego. When that happened, my terrorism task force friend became a hero, and I received an important promotion. Because of them, we were able to force the Ben-Meyers to cut a deal for their much sought-after clients—well-known international criminals to whom they'd sold new identities. They told us how they moved their ill-found money and how they reinvested the laundered money. It became a very important investigation.

"Callie and Cash never told me about the specifics of what they'd done. We agreed that under the circumstances, it would be best if I didn't know the details. I did know that Callie had saved Cash's life, though I never knew how. What I'll always remember is my interchange with Callie at her restaurant when it was all over.

"Callie came up to me and said, 'I apologize for disappearing on you, but Cash's life was at stake. Please forgive me.'

"And I'll never forget my response... 'You're forgiven...dear God, I missed who he was, completely...I understand now why you'd absolutely have to save this quiet man's life...'

"More than three years later, I feel that even more. He's a remarkable man, who doesn't draw attention to his accomplishments, to his unusual gifts and capacities, and I'm honored to be his friend."

After another round of applause, people began singing "Happy Birthday" again.

Sara came over and put Young Cash on Cash's lap. He was feeling good about this unexpected celebration, but plainly just having his grandson on his lap was an additional special treat. When the chorus of "Happy Birthday" was over, he sang little nothings to Baby Cash, then passed him back to Callie.

Sara, who was standing over him, raised her glass when he finished cooing.

"I'm the one who started this process of creating truly safe lives for our family as a prerequisite to staying together. We're still working on it, and it's a difficult thing to figure out. I'm more committed than ever to finding a solution, and I believe we will. Whatever we end up doing, there's something I want to say about my dad on his fiftieth birthday..." She took a beat, looking around at all of the people around the fire. "My dad did a very difficult, quite amazing thing for me. And because he is who he is, he did it simply, seemingly effortlessly, and without me knowing what he did until it was already done... Put simply, he brought me back to life...in his unassuming way, he taught me how to live again. My wonderful husband, my remarkable baby, my new family—Callie,

Lew, the Macher, and Andre—my relationships with all of you here on the beach around this fire, none of this could have happened without him." Sara put her hands on Cash's shoulder.

The cheers were deafening. Callie, the Macher, even Andre, had tears in their eyes.

Baby Cash, who liked being next to Grandpa, had sat back down with Callie on his blanket next to Cash's feet. When he finished his bottle, Cash opened a little toy box that he kept handy for the occasion, and Baby Cash picked out three toys, and he was happily busy again.

When it quieted down, people helped themselves to more hors d'oeuvres and refreshed their drinks. Corey Logan stood.

"I have a story to tell about my husband, Abe. I'm new to this obviously unusual group, but I'm telling this story because, Cash, in so many important ways, is like Abe. It's a story about unconventional, capable outsiders, people able to seemingly effortlessly do extremely difficult things. Though they couldn't be more different in their backgrounds, or in their work, both of those singular, distinctive men share these qualities. It was very hard for me to understand Abe, even though my very life depended on it. Because of that experience, though, I think I get it about Cash, and I'd like to use this story to explain why… It's a story that happened right here," she pointed to the house and the blackberry brambles on the edge of the field that sprawled almost fifty yards across the bluff. "It was more than ten years ago. I was hiding, afraid for my life and my son's life. Abe had found me, asked me, even pushed me, to confront my worst enemy, my nemesis, Nick Season. Abe wanted me to come back with him to Seattle and to marry him there, in my own house, my own backyard. I had to say no to all of those things."

Corey took a beat; this was important. "We decided to spend some time away together, not quite the same as what you're doing, but not unrelated. So we were here, the three of us, taking a little respite. We'd just had lunch. After lunch, I said to Abe and my fifteen-year-old son, Billy, 'If you pick some blackberries, I'll make a pie.' I even told them, 'Make a lot of noise so you won't surprise a bear.' Then I watched them from the window, singing loud scare-the-bear-songs and filling their pails. Soon after, I saw Billy slip, then I saw his pail of berries fly through the air, and I heard him screaming. I flew out the door, down the porch steps onto the field where I could see Billy near the brambles, flailing his arms wildly at swarming insects. I put it together instantly: Billy had fallen on a wasp's nest, yellow jackets that commonly build their nests in the ground. And now, the wasps were everywhere, and Billy was covered with stinging yellow jackets. I ran toward him, yelling incoherently, beside myself, unsure what to do. And then, out of nowhere, there was Abe, hauling Billy over his shoulder and running like hell across the field. They came charging out of the field onto the bluff's rocky edge, both of them covered with yellow jackets now, and without breaking stride, Abe jumped into the freezing cold water with Billy slung over his shoulder.

"I ran to the edge of the bluff. When they came up for air, I could see that the wasps were gone. Billy was having trouble breathing; I could hear him gasping for air. Abe was flailing in the cold salt water of the deep glacially gauged inlet. He was being carried out into the deeper water.

"That's when I remembered that Abe couldn't swim. I dove from the bluff into the icy water. And I decided to marry Abe."

There was wild cheering, raised glasses, and thunderous applause.

After a beat, Corey smiled, then said, "There's more. That night after dinner, I announced, 'I have something to say.' I raised my glass, a toast, 'First to the two best men I know.' I touched Billy's glass, then Abe's. I turned to Abe. 'My next toast is a little more complicated. It took me a while to get this. I finally saw it this afternoon. It was when you grabbed Billy the way you did, then jumped in the ocean, even though you couldn't swim. I mean, you had no chance at all—none—of getting to shore on your own. But I believe that somehow you knew that I'd get you out of the water safe. One way or another. And you were absolutely right. When I dove off that cliff, I knew I was not going to let you drown. No way. And I think that's what you've been trying to tell me—that if we go back, you're going to get me to shore. One way or another. That you know you can do that. And for reasons that I can't put into words, I believe I can count on you. Well, only a fool would walk away from that.' I clicked our raised glasses. 'Abe, I'd like to be your wife, if you'll still have me.'"

Another loud roar of cheering and applause. When it died down, Corey continued, "I'd been afraid to go back to Seattle, and I'd been resisting Abe's proposal of marriage. That ended at that moment, right here," she pointed at the house on the bluff. "The rest of our lives began here, at this very special place. The reason I told this very personal story is because from what I've seen and heard, in some unexpected ways, Cash reminds me of Abe. He's understated, unassuming, startlingly capable, nothing at all what he's supposed to be… Most importantly, like Abe, he's comfortably unconventional, put another way—he's well outside the mainstream and comfortable living in that skin. And I hope I'm not betraying a confidence, but if ever there's been an appropriate moment for that, it's now. I can say, both from my own life and on reliable advice, that some very special women love men like this."

Callie turned red. Sara laughed out loud.

"This capable, lovely man deserves a fine, long life with his family. I'd like to help make that happen."

Cash and Callie came and simultaneously embraced Corey. It was a long, lingering hug. Everyone applauded it.

After it ended, and there was a quiet moment, Abe raised a glass, "My wonderful wife never ceases to amaze me… Bravo, Corey." and when the cheers subsided yet again, "I can say easily from my special vantage point, that Cash is everything that all of you have said. As his therapist, there are limitations on what I can say. However, within those restraints, I can honestly say that he's a man who brings out the very best in the people around him. He's done that for me, and, I'm sure, for all of you."

There was more celebration, more well wishes all around. Everyone took a turn, even Andre.

It was quiet then, as everyone savored this very special time. Everyone there knew that they were in the presence of an unusual man, a man who had touched all of them.

That's when Callie handed the baby to Sara, then stood. She raised her recently filled martini, waited until she had everyone's attention, then began tentatively, "To the man of my dreams. I love him very much…" She paused, looking carefully around this place, these people, then looked at Cash, taking a breath. "Here comes the hard part…" She took a good long sip of her drink, then she looked Cash straight in the eye. "Cash Logan, will you marry me?"

Cash stood, then looked back into Callie's eyes, "Dear God…Callie James…I thought you'd never ask."

Callie's expression changed, first relief, and then excitement. "Really? With all of your heart?"

"I've longed for this…" He touched his glass to hers.

When she calmed down, she took another sip of her drink, clicked Cash's martini again, then set her own down carefully. She made a pleased face, "Well, I don't know how I knew this, but I knew it had to be me. After I heard Corey's story, I couldn't wait another moment. I do so want to be your wife, you can't imagine."

"I foolishly thought you didn't want to remarry. In all of this wonderful praise for me, someone, say Andre, who I know would have enjoyed doing this, could have pointed out how I often miss what's right in front of my eyes."

Andre cried out, "Yes, always!"

Cash raised his glass to his friend, set it down, then turned to Callie. "In this case, it's what I wanted more than anything else. Can we do it now, before you change your mind?"

"How?"

"Itzac, aren't you able to marry us?"

"I am ordained, and it would be my pleasure," the Macher replied. "After our marvelous dinner, I can marry you right here, on the beach."

"Perfect!" Callie replied. "I'd like Sara and Lew as witnesses."

Sara and Lew cried out, "Yes," simultaneously.

"Done," Cash said.

"In Yiddish," the Macher nodded, firm.

"Yes, absolutely," Andre insisted. "Mazel tov."

Abe stood, raised his glass, "L'chaim…to life."

Cash took Callie's hand, then motioned to Sara, who joined holding hands with them, along with Alvaro, who held Baby Cash's hand. Callie brought Lew beside her. All five of them held their hands together raised high, then they graciously bowed, heads down, to the others, in unison. They raised their heads and hands high, yet again.

Cash and Callie stepped forward. He called out, "Thank you, my dear, dear friends!"

Callie raised her hand with his, then joyously together, they called, "Bravo! Thank you! Bravo!"

The crowd roared, then shouted out, triumphant, "L'Chayim… to life."

Acknowledgments

Tyson Cornell, Jacob Epstein, Ruth Grant, Guy Intoci, Brendan Kiley, John McCaffrey, Megan Mintchev, Bob Weissbourd, Dorothy Escribano Weissbourd, Emily Weissbourd, and Rick Weissbourd.

www.ingramcontent.com/pod-product-compliance
Lightning Source LLC
Chambersburg PA
CBHW010201100726
47947CB00009B/42

* 9 7 8 1 6 4 4 2 8 4 4 0 7 *